Song of the Dolphin Boy

*Books by Elizabeth Laird published
by Macmillan Children's Books*

Welcome to Nowhere
Dindy and the Elephant
The Fastest Boy in the World
The Prince Who Walked with Lions
The Witching Hour
Lost Riders
Crusade
Oranges in No Man's Land
Paradise End
Secrets of the Fearless
A Little Piece of Ground
The Garbage King
Jake's Tower
Red Sky in the Morning
Kiss the Dust

Song of the Dolphin Boy

Fountaindale Public Library
Bolingbrook, IL
(630) 759-2102

Illustrated by Peter Bailey

Elizabeth Laird

MACMILLAN CHILDREN'S BOOKS

First published 2018 by Macmillan Children's Books
an imprint of Pan Macmillan
20 New Wharf Road, London N1 9RR
Associated companies throughout the world
www.panmacmillan.com

ISBN 978-1-5098-2823-4

Text copyright © Elizabeth Laird 2018
Illustrations copyright © Peter Bailey 2018

The right of Elizabeth Laird and Peter Bailey to be identified as the
author and illustrator of this work has been asserted by them in
accordance with the Copyright, Designs and Patents Act 1988.

All rights reserved. No part of this publication may be reproduced,
stored in a retrieval system, or transmitted, in any form or by any means
(electronic, mechanical, photocopying, recording or otherwise),
without the prior written permission of the publisher.

Pan Macmillan does not have any control over, or any responsibility for,
any author or third-party websites referred to in or on this book.

1 3 5 7 9 8 6 4 2

A CIP catalogue record for this book is available from
the British Library.

Printed and bound by CPI Group (UK) Ltd, Croydon CR0 4YY

This book is sold subject to the condition that it shall not,
by way of trade or otherwise, be lent, resold, hired out,
or otherwise circulated without the publisher's prior consent
in any form of binding or cover other than that in which
it is published and without a similar condition including this
condition being imposed on the subsequent purchaser.

For Ralph, Bertie and Leila

The Lighthouse

The School

The Lambs' House

The Shop

The Beach

A fisherman sat on the lonely shore,
Mending his nets and sighing.
Far out to sea, a dolphin heard
The love song he was singing.

She swam like an arrow, straight and true
And out from the water did run.
No dolphin now! A woman fair,
Her hair from pure gold spun!

The fisherman's heart beat fast with joy
And he set her on his knee.
She twined her arms around his neck.
'I'll marry you,' said she.

He took her to his little house
High on the cliffs above.
She bore a child, a little boy,
And her heart was filled with love.

The summer passed, and the winter passed,
And the summer came once more.
The dolphin woman sighed and said,
'My heart is weary and sore.

'O, I am a woman on the land
And a dolphin in the sea.
A miraculous child, a magical child,
Is the son that is born to me.

'I hear my people calling, calling,
And I must go back to the sea.
Though I love my man and my baby dear
They will never more see me.'

Chapter One

It all began at Dougie Lamb's eighth birthday party. It wasn't a big party. In fact there were only four other children at it, including Dougie's older sister, Kyla. Mrs Lamb, Dougie's mum, had been so excited about organizing her darling boy's party that she'd have invited a hundred and fifty children, if there'd been a hundred and fifty children to invite.

But Stromhead was a very small village in a far-off corner of Scotland, and there were only a few houses clustered round the harbour, along with a tiny school and a lighthouse up on the cliff top. And there weren't any other children from the village to ask. Except for Finn. But nobody ever invited Finn to anything.

Kyla and Mrs Lamb were both small, with loads of

smooth blonde hair, and they both liked everything to be pretty and perfect. 'Sweet' was their favourite word, followed by 'cute'. Kyla's dad called them 'my sugarplums'. He worked on the oil rigs out at sea and was often away from home. Dougie missed him dreadfully. Mr Lamb would never have given him a kitten jigsaw puzzle for his birthday, like Kyla had, which was *nearly* as bad as the little Prince Charming outfit from his mum. No, Dougie's dad gave him useful, interesting things, like sets of spanners, and a chain with a padlock and key. Dougie had adored them as soon as he'd seen them. This was a grown-up present; something useful. He could stop things from opening and tie things down. It made him feel in control. In fact, the padlock and chain were Dougie's favourite possessions of all time.

Kyla and Mrs Lamb had been fussing round all morning getting ready for the party, and at last the little gold clock on the mantelpiece in the sitting room struck a tinkly three chimes. It was time for the other children to arrive.

In fact, they were walking slowly up the road towards the Lambs' cottage, grumbling all the way.

'I never wanted to go to this stupid party, anyway,' Charlie groaned. He was short and stocky, with a head as hard and round as a cannon-ball. 'Knowing Dougie's mum, it'll be all soft and stupid and babyish. And, anyway, my dad was going to take me out fishing in my own wee boat this afternoon.'

Amir grunted in sympathy.

'And I'd just got to the next level in my game,' he said with a sigh. 'Mum only lets me play on my computer on Saturday afternoons. I'll have to wait a whole week now!'

Amir shifted his glasses up his nose with one long slim finger. His forehead, under a heavy fringe of black hair, was creased in a frown. Jas looked at him sympathetically. Amir's mum, Mrs Faridah, was their class teacher, and very strict.

'Well,' she said, trying to be fair. 'At least there'll be a cake and everything. Anyway, Dougie can't help it that there aren't any other kids of his age around.'

Charlie scowled at her.

'Why do you have to be so stupid and *nice* all the time?'

She crossed her dark eyes, stuck her tongue out at him, pushed her thumbs into her ears and waggled the rest of her hands. Her freckled face looked so funny, framed by bouncing brown hair, that Amir burst out laughing, and even Charlie had to grin.

The three of them, along with Kyla and Dougie, had known each other almost since they were born, and Jas had learned years ago that it was pointless to rise to Charlie's bait.

They were almost at the Lambs' cottage when Amir hissed, 'Watch out! There's Finn!'

Finn, the only other person in their tiny class in the village's little school, was walking along the road in front of them with his hands thrust deep into his pockets, his shoulders hunched unhappily. He had also known the other children all his life, but they had always avoided him. There was just something about Finn – the way his pale brown hair was slicked so smoothly back from his forehead, perhaps, or the sad aura of loneliness that clung to him – that made the other children feel uneasy.

Charlie was actually enraged by him, but then Charlie was like a firework anyway. Just the sight of Finn was enough to set him off into a massive shower of sparks.

'He's not going to the party too, is he?' he spluttered. 'That's it. I'm going home.'

But before he could turn round, Finn had slouched on past the Lambs' cottage and disappeared round a bend in the road. Amir and Jas watched him go, feeling guilty and relieved at the same time. Then Jas led the way up to the Lambs' front door and pressed the bell. Kyla rushed to open it before the chimes had even died away, and the three guests went reluctantly inside.

There was a bit too much of everything in the Lambs' house. The cushions on the flowery sofa were too soft, the door chimes were too musical, the bow round the neck of Buttons (the kitten) was too baby-blue, and there were too many frills on the curtains.

Nobody realized that Finn, who had seen the three children on their way to the party, had eventually doubled back to see what was going on. He was standing outside in the garden, glaring into the living room, and shredding Mrs Lamb's prize roses one by one to leave a scatter of pink petals on the grass.

'They never let me in on *anything*,' Finn muttered to himself. 'They're all mean and horrible, and I wouldn't be friends with them even if they asked me.'

He knew, though, that the last bit wasn't true. Finn longed to have friends more than anything else in the world. He didn't particularly want to be a computer genius, like Amir, work in a pet shop, like Kyla, or be a footballer, like Charlie. He didn't want to be a mechanic, like Dougie, or even the prime minister, like Jasmine. He only wanted to be a friend.

Curiosity had brought him back to spy on the party, which Dougie had been going on about for weeks. Finn had known that it might feel like torture to

look in from the outside, but he hadn't been able to resist.

As he watched, though, a slow smile spread over his face. The party wasn't going well at all. In fact, it was awful.

Mrs Lamb's idea of a children's party had got stuck

somewhere around the year when Dougie was four. The children were being forced to endure Pass the Parcel, Simon Says and The Farmer's in his Den. Finn nearly laughed out loud at the sight of Charlie, whose temper was about to boil over anyway and who hated being kept indoors, pretending to be the farmer's horse. He looked like a tiger about to spring.

He'll bite someone in a minute, with a bit of luck, Finn thought bitterly. *I really hope he does. I hope he freaks out and breaks something. I hope he smashes the place up.*

Amir, who was dying to get home to his computer game and had been chewing his lip with frustration, was now yawning till his jaw ached, while Jasmine kept looking at the cuckoo clock on the wall. She was obviously wondering why the hands were going round so slowly. Even Dougie, the birthday boy himself, was looking more and more anxious. Only Kyla seemed to be enjoying herself. She had given up joining in with the games and was playing with Buttons the cat.

'Teatime!' sang out Dougie's mum, whisking away the cloth that had been hiding everything laid out on the table.

Finn's mouth had widened into a broad grin as he'd watched the party fall apart, but the sight of the tea spread out on the table wiped it off his face. He would have given anything to have piled up a plate with all the treats that Mrs Lamb had prepared. He looked them over longingly. There were little sandwiches cut into triangles, butterfly cookies, cupcakes with mounds of icing on top, and mini sausage rolls. His mouth watered so much, he had to swallow. He was just about to turn away, unable to torture himself any longer, when he heard Dougie's mum say, 'Why don't you save some for your friend Finn? What a pity he couldn't come.' Then she went out into the kitchen to fetch another plate of biscuits.

Charlie stared at Dougie, disgusted.

'You invited *Finn*?'

Dougie laughed nervously. He was nearly three years younger than Charlie and looked up to him with a mixture of fear and admiration.

'Mum made me write the invitation, but I didn't give it to him, honestly, Charlie.'

Finn's fists tightened.

One day, I'm going to sort Charlie out. I'm going to . . . he thought, but he stopped, unable to think of anything bad enough to do to his tormentor. Then he saw Jas's face. She was frowning at Dougie, as if she thought he'd been mean.

She's the only one who's worth anything, Finn told himself grudgingly.

Dougie, realizing that his party was going wrong, was desperately counting on the big moment that would put everything right.

'Wait till you see my cake,' he babbled. 'Mum made it herself. It's a special shape. It's going to be a surprise. I think it's going to be a dinosaur.'

'Yeah, a pretty little dino-baby with a bow round its neck,' sneered Charlie.

'I bet it'll be lovely, Dougie,' Jas said kindly.

'I don't care what it looks like as long as it's chocolate,' said Amir.

Jas turned to say something to him, and was suddenly facing the window. Finn ducked down quickly behind the rose bush, out of sight.

When at last Mrs Lamb brought the cake out of the kitchen and placed it carefully down in the middle of the table, Finn nearly laughed out loud. It wasn't a dinosaur, and it wasn't even chocolate. It was in the shape of a cat, with the eyes made of sparkly silver balls, and a blue bow tied round its neck.

Dougie's face went red.

'Mum!' he wailed. 'It's *pink*!'

Charlie snorted. Amir sniggered. Jasmine bit her lip, feeling sorry for Dougie. Kyla clapped her hands.

'It's lovely, Mum,' she said. 'Can I have the tail?'

Finn couldn't remember the last time he'd had a piece of cake. He wanted to burst in through the window, grab the whole thing, and run off with it. Instead, he watched as the candles were lit and Dougie blew them out. His mouth watered all over again as Mrs Lamb cut the cake and handed out the pieces. He knew he ought to go, before he started to feel too lonely, but he couldn't tear himself away.

When the cake was half demolished, and everyone's mouth was sticky with pink icing, Charlie said loudly, 'Can we go now? My dad'll have brought the boat in. He needs me to help unload the lobster pots.'

'Not yet, dear,' cooed Dougie's mum. 'I've had a sweet idea. Now here's a piece of coloured paper and a felt tip each. I want every one of you to write some birthday wishes to Dougie. Then we'll tie them to the balloons and let them go up into the sky where the birds can read them and send Dougie birthday messages too.'

'Mum, no! *Mum!*' wailed Dougie.

'I wouldn't want a bird's message landing on my head, birthday message or no birthday message,' said Charlie.

The others burst out laughing.

'Specially not a great big seagull's,' said Amir.

'No need to be *crude*, boys. I'm sure you can think of something lovely to write,' said Mrs Lamb, frowning.

'What, you mean like "Dougie you are a sweet, cute, ducky wee baa-lamb, coochie-coo"?' Charlie whispered to Jasmine.

She dug him in the ribs, trying not to laugh.

'How do you spell "gorgeous"?' said Amir, winking at Jas.

Dougie looked as if he was going to be sick.

A few minutes later, Finn had to dash out quickly through the garden gate as the children burst out of the house like champagne fizzing out of a bottle. He scrambled up the hill above the village, ignoring the gorse that scratched his legs, and watched as a clutch of brightly coloured balloons were lifted by the breeze out of the hands of the children.

With their strings trailing behind them, they floated up and away, skimming the chimneys of the old fishermen's cottages, sailing over the roof of the school, where Mrs Faridah, Amir's mother, was writing reports, above the village shop where Mrs Lamb worked during the week. They glided past the tall white tower of the lighthouse, where Professor Jamieson, Jasmine's father, was writing busily at his desk, and across the harbour, where Charlie's dad was unloading his lobster pots. Then they drifted out to sea, sinking lower as the air hissed out of them, until they landed on the choppy water and bobbed up and down like brightly coloured flowers.

For some reason, the sight of them made Finn shudder. Reluctantly, he made his way home to the tumbledown cottage along the cliff top where he lived with his dad. He didn't look back as he walked up the hill, but if he had, he'd have seen Mrs Lamb standing in her garden looking down in puzzlement at the mass of torn rose petals all over her neatly mown lawn.

Chapter Two

Finn and his dad lived on their own in an ancient cottage perched on the cliff top beyond Stromhead. It was so old that it looked as if it had grown up out of the ground by itself like a monstrous mushroom. The weeds in the cottage's garden had sprouted so high that they almost covered the windows, which no one ever cleaned anyway, so it was very dark inside. There would have been a magnificent view from the windows if Finn and his dad had only been able to see out of them, but it was just as good from the garden gate. Finn loved to stand there, looking across the road at the steep, narrow path that wound down to the beach below, and the tumble of rocks at the edge of the sand, which ran out into the sea. He could never get enough of gazing out across the water, which turned a new colour every day.

Sometimes it was such an intense blue that you couldn't tell where the sea ended and the sky began, and at other times it was a mysterious grey, making you wonder what secrets it held in its watery depths. He liked it best at night, when the surface was a rippling, shining black, and the moon cast a silvery path across the water.

He had to make do with looking, though, because his father had absolutely forbidden him ever to go down the steep, rough-hewn steps that led to the little cove below. Mr McFee had always looked so angry at the thought of his son going near the water's edge that Finn shrank inside every time he thought about it.

One day, maybe, he'll let me go, he told himself. *Or perhaps I'll just sneak down there when he's not looking.*

But he knew he never would.

He had often wondered why his father hated the sea so much, why he never went near the harbour or the beach, and why, whenever he came home, he would turn his back on the view as soon as he could, closing the door with a snap behind him as if to shut out the sea.

Mr McFee's feelings about the sea were just one

of the many things that Finn didn't dare to talk to his father about. He'd tried when he was younger to ask him about his mother, who had disappeared when he was only two, but his dad had either erupted in a blaze of anger, sending Finn dashing out of the room in a panic, or he'd gone quiet and sad, making Finn feel guilty that he'd asked at all.

Mr McFee, in fact, was the saddest man in the village. He hadn't always been like that. He'd been a fisherman once, like Charlie's father, strong and handsome, with a great voice for music, and everything neat and

shipshape round him. He'd been singing one evening while he was mending his nets on the beach when a girl had swum up out of the sea and come up to him. Finn's dad had taken one look at her and his heart had bounded right out of his chest. The girl had fallen in love with him too. She'd gone home with him, listening all the way to his wonderful singing. Soon they were married, and then Finn was born. You could never have seen a happier man than Finn's dad then, though Finn's mum stayed close to the cottage on the cliffs and rarely went into the village.

But one day, when Finn was only two years old, his mother disappeared. She left nothing behind in the cottage (which had always been sparklingly clean and neat back then), except for a row of sea shells on the windowsill.

There had been a huge hunt for her all over Scotland, but she was never found. People began to look strangely at Finn's dad, and there were even whispers running round the village that he'd had something to do with her disappearance. Mr McFee stopped bothering to go out fishing. He stopped cleaning and tidying the house, or even cleaning and tidying himself. He spent hours sitting in a sagging old chair with his back to the window, ignoring Finn, who toddled around on his own.

Finn had brought himself up without much help from his dad. Every now and then, Mr McFee would come back from the store in Stromhead with a bag of food and some cans of beer, and sometimes he noticed that Finn's clothes were too small for him and he'd find some second-hand ones from somewhere or other.

It wasn't that he didn't love Finn. Sometimes he'd get up out of his greasy old chair, pick Finn up, holding him too tight, and say embarrassing things like, 'You're all I've got, Finn! You won't ever leave me like *she* did, will you?' Finn would wriggle away as fast as he could and run out of the cottage, leaving his dad slouched in his chair once more with tears trickling down his face.

People muttered when the McFees went past, and crossed to the other side of the street. Finn was used to seeing suspicion and rejection in every closed face he passed. Stromhead was a gossipy place, where everyone was interested in their neighbours' business. Finn knew that people found them strange, but no one had ever told him that they thought his dad was a murderer.

Finn couldn't remember anything about his mum, except for one thing. She had whistled while she'd rocked him to sleep, and the sound was so beautiful, so clear and haunting, that he had never forgotten it. It made him think of the distant *shh shh* of waves rippling on the beach below the cliff. He'd learned to whistle himself when he was only five years old. It was a private thing for Finn, and he did it only when he was alone. In his secret heart, he hoped that by whistling he might call his mother back to him. But she never came.

It was a few days after Dougie's party, and Finn, with the usual feeling of sullen dread in his heart, was getting ready to go to school.

Only two more days to get through before the weekend, he told himself, rummaging round in his schoolbag to check if he'd put his homework in it. He felt something at the bottom, and fished out a note from Mrs Faridah. His heart sank as he glanced through it. He'd been dreading giving it to his father, but with the holiday looming, he had no choice. He put it into his dad's hand.

'It's from school, Dad. It's about swimming lessons. There's a minibus going to take my class to the pool in Rothiemuir. All the others are going. You're supposed to give me the money today.'

His father looked at him blankly.

'What letter? Give it here.'

Mr McFee stared at the crumpled paper in his hand; then he stared at his son.

'What's this load of tripe?' he said. 'Swimming? Pounds and pounds they want. Just for a bunch of kids to paddle around in some water! It's a disgrace!'

'Do you mean you won't pay?' said Finn, not at all surprised.

'It's not *won't* pay, son; it's *can't* pay,' said Mr McFee, scratching at the bald spot on top of his head. 'It's one thing after another at that school of yours. Uniform, shoes, a schoolbag – what do they think I am? A millionaire?'

His voice had started low, but it was beginning to rise ominously.

'Mrs Faridah said we'd have to have swimming costumes too,' said Finn in a small voice.

Mr McFee banged his fist down on the arm of the chair.

'Whatever next? They want you flying off to the moon? They want me buying you a spacesuit?' He wagged a grubby finger in front of Finn's face, making Finn back away. 'I won't have it, do you hear? I won't have you going swimming at all. Deep water's a killer. It's what took her. I've told you before, a hundred times – you've not to go near the beach, and if ever I catch you down at the harbour, I'll . . .'

He was working himself up into a froth of anger, but Finn was no longer listening. What was that his father had said? The sea had taken *her*? Did he mean Finn's mother? Had she drowned? Was that why his father hated the thought of deep water so much, and would never let him go down to the beach?

It wasn't until his father was by the door, putting on his boots, that Finn started listening again.

'*I'll* tell that Mrs Faridah!' Mr McFee was saying. 'I'll go down to the school myself and get it sorted. I'll . . .'

Finn jumped with fright.

'It's all right, Dad. You don't need to,' he said hastily. 'I'll just explain that I'm not allowed.'

He held his breath, watching his father's face. The last time his dad had burst into the school, he'd stood ranting away at Mrs Faridah in front of all the other children, who'd sat giggling behind their hands. In the end, Mrs Faridah had had to call the caretaker to take him out through the school gates. Finn had been so embarrassed, he'd wanted to die.

To Finn's relief, his father kicked his boots off again and subsided back into the chair, his anger gone.

'Mind you do, son. You stand up to them. No swimming, do you hear? It's you I'm worried about. I only want what's best for you. You know that, don't you?'

'I know, Dad. I know,' Finn said sadly, watching his father's face fall again into its usual sadness. He'd known he wouldn't be allowed to go in the minibus with the others, but he'd allowed himself to hope.

He sidled past his father, stepped out through the front door, and began to run along the cliff top towards the village. He hated being late for school. He liked to get into the classroom first, and to be sitting quietly in his corner before the others came tumbling in. The best thing was not to be noticed at all.

Heavy summer rain was falling by the time he arrived at school. His dad had never got around to buying him a raincoat or boots, but the rain didn't bother Finn. He hardly noticed it.

Stromhead Primary School was big and spacious, but the classrooms were half empty. Years ago the village had been full of children, the sons and daughters of fishermen, farmers and the families who ran the pub and the shops in the village. But nearly all the fishermen had gone now. The only trawler left in the harbour belonged to Charlie's dad, who used it for lobster potting. The shops had closed too, except for the General Store where Mrs Lamb worked. There had been some incomers to the village, like Jas's dad, Professor Jamieson, who had moved into the lighthouse, which had stopped working years ago. Amir and his parents too had settled in Stromhead from Pakistan, though Amir's father worked in Aberdeen for a ferry company and rarely came home.

There were only eleven children in the school altogether, split into two classes. The five little ones in the Infants were in a separate building on the other side of the playground, and the remaining six were in Mrs Faridah's Juniors class. They were Charlie, Jas, Amir, Kyla, Finn and Dougie. Charlie, Amir and Jas were eleven, and Kyla was ten. Dougie was only eight, but he was too old to be with the little ones, and he had to struggle along with the others as best he could. Finn was eleven too, but he seemed somehow older than the three older ones, and at the same time younger than the younger children. He didn't quite fit in with anyone. Mrs Faridah kept trying her best to help him join in with the class, but Finn was so used to being by himself that he was as relieved as the other children when he was allowed to go back to being on his own.

He was watching warily now as Charlie blustered into the classroom. He'd learned long ago that Charlie was like an energetic dog on rainy days. He hated being cooped up in a small space. It made him all twitchy and ready to snap. The best thing was to avoid him.

Today Charlie looked more thunderous than even a wet day could explain. Finn couldn't know, of course, that Charlie had dropped his toast on the floor at breakfast time, sticky side down, his big sister had laughed at him and called him a butterfingers, and his dad had growled something that he wished he hadn't heard. Then he'd stubbed his toe really badly while running round the house looking for his second trainer, and trodden on the cat, who'd scratched him.

*

All day long, during wet break and wet lunchtime, Finn managed to keep out of Charlie's way. The afternoon was always the worst on rainy days. The children were bored and fed up with being indoors. Today things were even worse than usual, as the rain had found a hole in the roof, and water was coming into the classroom. It had dripped down the wall and ruined a picture of the Stromhead lighthouse that Finn had drawn. He'd been really proud of it too.

He spent the last half-hour of the day ignoring the rest of the class, sitting on his own, staring up at a poster that Mrs Faridah had pinned up on a dry bit of the classroom wall. It was about dolphins. There was one big picture in the middle of a dolphin leaping out of the water, with silvery drops catching the light against the blue of the sky, and lots of smaller pictures surrounding it of different kinds of dolphins, with maps and information about where they lived and what they did.

The poster fascinated Finn. As he looked at it, he felt as if he could almost see the streamlined creatures travelling for miles through the deep ocean, calling to each other with their calves by their sides, diving and playing, leaping in the foam, slapping their tails down on the water. The classroom grew dim as he imagined himself out there with them in the sea, the water running smoothly along his body, the calm presence of friends around him.

Mrs Faridah broke into his daydream.

'The school will have to be closed tomorrow, children, so that we can get this leak fixed,' she said. 'As it's a Friday, and there's a Bank Holiday on Monday, you've got a nice long weekend to look forward to.'

Finn groaned to himself. He never knew which was worse, the dread of going to school or the lonely emptiness of the holidays. On balance, he thought he really preferred going to school.

'Finn? Finn!' Jas was nudging him. 'Didn't you hear? It's your turn to put the books away. I'll help you if you like. And look, it's stopped raining at last. It's really nice out there now.'

Finn came to with a start. The end of the school day had come, and he hadn't even noticed it. She was right. The rain had stopped, and a bright square of sunlight shone through the classroom window on to the floor. He nodded at Jas awkwardly. He could tell that she was trying to be nice to him.

It's only because she's feeling guilty about the party, he thought grudgingly. But he knew that wasn't fair.

Jas was the only one who did talk to him sometimes. She'd even volunteered to do a project with him once, on the Romans, though he could tell she'd been relieved when it was over.

The others were collecting their things and making for the door. Finn hastily gathered up all the books that had been lying on the tables, and Jas took them from him and put them back on the shelf. Then, still half in a dream, he picked up his bag and went towards the door.

'Here, Finn – you've forgotten your homework,' Jas said, picking up a sheet of paper that he'd left on his desk and handing it to him.

He stared at it.

'Weren't you listening? It's the poem we've got to learn over the weekend. You know – the one Mrs Faridah was talking about. The selkie story.'

Finn started reading the poem as he walked slowly towards the classroom door – and as he read, something turned in his stomach.

> *A fisherman sat on the lonely shore,*
> *Mending his nets and sighing.*
> *Far out to sea, a dolphin heard*
> *The love song he was singing.*

> *She swam like an arrow, straight and true*
> *And out from the water did run.*
> *No dolphin now! A woman fair,*
> *Her hair from pure . . .*

He was so far away as he read, he forgot all about Charlie, whose temper had got worse and worse as the day had gone on. By now, after hours cooped up indoors, he was like a volcano, with hot rocks and steam and lava all bubbling around inside him, ready to burst out.

It was pure bad luck that Finn, still engrossed in the poem, happened to be walking past the classroom door just as Charlie tried to barge through it. Finn didn't move quickly enough, and Charlie gave him a shove. Finn, still in a dream, lost his balance and fell backwards, knocking over the table on which Mrs Faridah had set out a display of shells to start the class collection. They landed on the floor with a horrible crash, and some of the big old ones broke.

Finn gave a cry of distress. He loved shells. He liked to pick them up, look at their colours and stroke them, holding the big ones to his ear so that he could hear the sea. He was so upset, he forgot to be cautious. He stuffed the poem in his pocket and bent down to pick up the shells.

'Look what you've done, Charlie!' he blurted out. 'They're all broken.'

Charlie's eyes seemed to bulge out of his head.

'Look what *I've* done? Who knocked the table over? Who wouldn't get out of the way? Who's a sneaky wee – a sneaky, slimy . . .'

Mrs Faridah came hurrying out from the little staffroom to the side of the classroom.

'Charlie! What have you done now? I've had enough of you today. Look at this mess. My shells!'

The lava inside Charlie boiled right over.

'It wasn't me! It was him! Finn! I didn't touch your stupid table!'

'Finn?' said Mrs Faridah disbelievingly. 'I'm disappointed in you, Charlie. It's not like you to put the blame on someone else.'

It was the last straw.

'It's not fair! You always pick on me! It was Finn!' he shouted.

He stuck his face right into Finn's, and he looked so like a tiger, snarling and ferocious, that Finn gasped in panic. His heart beating wildly, he turned and darted out through the school door and began to run, through the gates and down the hill.

'Aagh!' roared Charlie, dashing after him. He was outside at last, and there, trying to escape, was the person who'd ruined his day. With the red mist clouding his eyes, every thought went out of Charlie's head except for the goal of catching his prey, and – and –

'Come on!' Jas yelled to the others. 'Charlie's in a rage! We've got to stop him before he does something awful!'

'He's going for Finn!' shrieked Kyla.

And leaving Mrs Faridah standing at the school door anxiously shaking her head, Jas, Amir, Kyla and Dougie raced after Charlie and Finn, the six of them streaking down the hill like a pack of hounds.

Finn didn't have any time to think about where he was going. The grass on the hillside beneath his flying feet gave way to the tarmac of the village street, then, suddenly, he was on the rough cobbles of the harbour wall. Too late, he realized that he'd made a terrible mistake. There was nothing ahead of him but the blunt end of the harbour wall and the sea beyond it. He was trapped.

He turned round. Charlie was almost on him.

'*You* knocked the shell table over!' Charlie was yelling. 'You made *me* get the blame! You . . . !'

Finn took a step backwards. Then another. And another. And then there was nothing beneath his feet. Arms and legs flailing, he fell off the harbour wall, down, down into the cold green sea.

Chapter Three

For a moment, Charlie was too shocked to do anything. His face, scarlet a moment ago, was turning a sickly white.

Jas came running up ahead of the other three.

'What have you done, Charlie? Where's Finn?'

'He – he fell into the sea,' stammered Charlie, and burst into tears.

Kyla gasped in fright.

'He can't swim! He'll drown!'

The others arrived.

'What's happened?' asked Amir.

Jas was peering down into the sea from the harbour wall. There were several little boats bobbing about near the steps that led down from the top of the wall to a little wooden platform below.

'Finn fell in,' she said shortly. 'I can't see him down there. He must be behind one of the boats.'

'Perhaps he's stuck,' said Kyla, who was always looking for disasters. 'Perhaps he's drowned, and his lifeless body will float out to sea and—'

Charlie gave a wail.

'You shouldn't have chased Finn, Charlie,' said Dougie reproachfully. 'You might've killed him.'

Charlie wrapped his arms round his head and sank down on to a bollard.

A clanking noise made Jas look up. On the far side of the harbour Charlie's dad was heaving lobster pots around on the deck on the *Janine*. Jas cupped her hands round her mouth.

'Mr Munro!' she shouted. 'Help! Finn's fallen into the sea. He can't swim!'

Mr Munro didn't hear. He went into the wheelhouse of the trawler and started up the engine.

'Shout louder, Jas,' said Kyla helpfully.

Charlie lifted his head.

'He's deaf. He can't hear you. It's all my fault. I'm a murderer. I'm . . .'

'What are you taking your shoes off for, Amir?' said Dougie.

Amir had kicked off his shoes, tucked his glasses

into one of them, and was throwing off his sweater. He didn't answer Dougie. He was already halfway down the steps towards the platform at the bottom.

Charlie jumped to his feet and began to wrestle his sweatshirt over his head.

'Come back, Amir! I told you, it's my fault! I'll go in,' he shouted.

Jas caught his collar in a strong grip.

'Let him go, Charlie. He's the best swimmer of all of us. He's done life-saving. You'll only get in his way.'

Charlie started to fight her off, but Dougie shouted, 'Look! Amir's jumped in!'

The four children leaned over the harbour wall again to look down. Amir was standing up to his chest in water between two small motor launches, looking surprised.

'It's really shallow here,' he called up to them. 'The tide's right out.'

'Can you see Finn?' Jas called back.

Amir didn't answer. He was wading round between the small boats, looking carefully behind and under each one.

'He must be down there somewhere,' Kyla shouted down to him. 'Are you sure he didn't knock himself out? Perhaps he's under the water. Perhaps he's already drowned.'

'Shut up, Kyla,' said Jas, seeing the look on Charlie's face. 'Of course he hasn't drowned. Amir would have seen him. We all would have.'

Amir appeared, dripping and breathless, at the top of the steps.

'I looked everywhere. All round the boats. He's not there. But he must be all right. It's so shallow that he wouldn't have needed to swim at all. He must have hidden behind a boat while we were all looking down. I bet he slipped out and went round to the beach while we were all arguing.'

The children looked at each other, anxiously wondering what to do. They couldn't see round the end of the harbour wall or over the far side of it on to the beach because of a rampart built up all along the length of the wall, which was made of rough-hewn stones with gaps in between them.

'I'll climb up and look,' said Amir.

Charlie pushed him aside. Without a word, he began to climb the rampart, while Amir put his shoes on and tried to wring some of the water out of his clothes.

'You're not allowed up there,' Dougie called up

to Charlie. 'You'll get into trouble.'

Charlie was nearly at the top of the wall when a bellow came from the *Janine*. Mr Munro had seen him.

'Get off that wall, you wee imp! *Now!*'

At the sound of his father's furious voice, Charlie lost his foothold and fell hard on to the cobbles. Jas ran across to him, trying to help him struggle to his feet.

'Are you all right, Charlie?' asked Kyla. 'I should think you've broken your leg.'

'Shut *up*, Kyla. I'm fine,' grunted Charlie, and he began to hobble after Jas and Dougie, who were already racing back along the cobbles to the tarmac road, with Amir squelching along behind them.

A few minutes later, the five of them were looking down the beach that ran behind the harbour wall, with its fringe of rocks beyond.

'There's no sign of him,' Jas said. 'It's like he's disappeared into thin air.'

'He's probably hiding over there in the rocks,' said Amir. 'There's loads of places.'

'Let's go and look,' said Jas. 'We can't just leave him. He might be hurt or — or anything.'

'You'd better not come, Charlie,' said Dougie. 'I bet if he sees you again, he'll think you still want to kill him.'

Kyla looked expectantly at Charlie, waiting for him to explode, but Charlie only glared at Dougie, then ran off to begin the search. Amir and Jas were already scrambling over the rocks, calling out, 'Finn! Finn, are you all right? Come out, Finn!'

The tumble of rocks on either side of the beach stuck far out into the water, and they were wet and slippery with seaweed.

There were plenty of places where a boy could hide, and the children worked hard, hunting in every crevice, calling out Finn's name, but there was no sign of him.

Dougie had to give up first, when his mother, on her way home from work at the village shop, caught sight of him scrambling over the rocks. She hurried down to the beach, calling out, 'Dougie, darling! Get down off those nasty rocks before you scratch yourselves to bits! Why aren't you at home?'

She was waiting on the sand as he jumped down from the rocks, and took hold of his arm in a tight grip. Dougie tried to wriggle free.

'No you don't,' she said firmly. 'You're coming home with me. Look at your feet! Soaking wet. You'll catch your death. Kyla, sweetie! Come on home!'

'Coming, Mum!' Kyla called back obediently. 'In a minute!' Then she jumped over to the next rock and went on hunting for Finn.

Mrs Lamb hesitated, then shouted, 'Well don't be long, darling. Don't be late for your tea!'

Kyla ignored her. Amir looked at her with grudging admiration. He wished he could get away with pretending to obey his mum, and then going on to do just what he liked, but Mrs Faridah was a lot tougher than Mrs Lamb. Anyway, it was Dougie that she really kept under her thumb. In a way, Amir felt a bit sorry for Dougie. He'd hate it if his mum treated him like a baby all the time.

It was obvious, when ten more minutes had passed, that Finn was nowhere in or on the rocks.

'We've hunted everywhere,' panted Jas, jumping down on to the sand. 'He's just not here.'

'He must have got out of the sea and run up off the beach as fast as a – as a cheetah,' said Amir, who liked watching wildlife films. 'It's weird. I don't know how he could have had the time.'

'Weird! Aye, that's Finn,' scoffed Charlie. 'He's weird all right.' And then, remembering that it had all been his fault anyway, and that he'd made himself a promise not to be nasty to Finn any more, his face went a dull red colour up to the roots of his spiky fair hair, and he started scuffing up sprays of sand with the toe of his shoe.

'We might as well give up and go home, I suppose,' said Jas, throwing one last anxious look round the beach.

They began to walk silently up towards the narrow road that separated the shore from the little village above the harbour. When they reached it, Jas suddenly stopped.

'We ought to do something about Finn,' she said. 'It's not fair, the way we've treated him. Keeping him out of Dougie's party and everything.'

'I know, but . . .' began Kyla.

'I mean, how would you like it?' said Jas.

'It's not as if . . .' began Amir, but then his voice tailed away.

'Jas is right,' said Charlie unwillingly. 'We – I mean *I've* got to stop being mean to him.'

A bellow from the harbour made his head whip round. Mr Munro was standing beside his pile of lobster pots, waving his arms furiously.

'I've got to go,' Charlie said hastily. 'My dad's going to do his nut. I was meant to be on the pots with him this afternoon.'

'Tomorrow, then,' said Jas hastily. 'We've got the day off anyway. Let's have a meeting. At the lighthouse. Ten o'clock. We'll make a plan and decide what to do.'

'Won't you have to ask your dad first?' asked Kyla curiously.

'Dad'll be working. He won't even notice we're there,' said Jas with a grin.

Chapter Four

Finn had been scared many times in his life before, but he had never experienced the sheer terror that overcame him when Charlie began to chase him. His heart had pounded so hard that he could hear it like a drumbeat in his ears. He felt like a rabbit running from a fox.

As he stepped back into the air, away from Charlie's snarling face, panic possessed him. He had time to think, *I can't swim! I'll drown!* And then he hit the water. He just missed hitting one of the small motor launches that were bobbing around at the bottom of the harbour steps. The wave he made swung the boat round so that he was behind it and hidden from the view of the children, who, seconds later, were looking down from the top.

In all his life, Finn had never been immersed in water. He'd never swum in a pool or wallowed in a bath or paddled in the sea. The shock took his breath away. The tide was so far out that although the water came up to his shoulders, his feet were still touching the bottom. He clutched at the bollard hanging off the side of the boat, and for a moment the cold seemed to paralyse him.

But the fear of Charlie was still on him.

He's not scared of water. He'll come down here and find me and . . . and . . . he told himself. *I've got to get away.*

He peered cautiously round the edge of the boat and looked up. He could hear Jas calling out to Mr Munro, and the muffled voices of the others, but their heads had disappeared. Then he waded in frantic haste to the steps that ran down from the harbour wall, making for a little wooden platform where no one would see him from above. He could hide there and wait until the other children had gone away, and then climb out and go home.

Feet thundered down the wooden steps overhead as Finn shrank back into the shadow under the platform. There was a loud splash as Amir jumped into the water, and Finn ducked right down until only his head was above the water. Holding his breath, he heard Amir calling up to the others, and their replies, and he only let it out when Amir hauled himself back on to the little wooden platform and ran back up the steps.

When he was quite sure that the coast was clear, he emerged shivering with cold and fright from underneath the wooden platform, took hold of the edge of it and tried to haul himself up. But the platform was slimy with seaweed. His hands slipped off it. He fell back into the water, which closed right over his head.

For a long, terrible moment, Finn thrashed with his arms and legs, trying to find solid ground to stand on, but then, almost at once, something changed. Something was happening to him – something strange and terrifying.

I must be drowning, he thought. *This is what it's like to drown.*

Somehow, he didn't mind.

I suppose my mum felt like this, he told himself. *Maybe she's doing this to me. Maybe she's waiting for me on – on the other side.*

He stopped struggling and felt peaceful and calm. He was floating, all of his body submerged in the water. It didn't even feel cold any more. The swell washed round him softly as if it was welcoming him. It seemed almost to hold him in an embrace. Without even trying, he raised his face till it broke the surface and took a long, deep breath. Then he let himself sink again, feeling a strange, new kind of energy flowing in his veins.

If I'm still breathing, I suppose I can't be dead, he thought dreamily. But it didn't seem to matter. Nothing mattered, except for the wonderful sensation of the water.

Something brushed against his leg. He twisted his head down to look. It was a little fish, which had darted away already. But now he made another discovery. He could see a long way through the clear, green water. Seaweed waved gracefully against the harbour wall. Small fish darted past him. He could hear things too, as if his ears had never worked properly before. On the far side of the harbour, the rumble of the *Janine*'s engine as Mr Munro started it up was shockingly loud. It masked the rustling, swishing noise of ripples brushing against the stones of the harbour wall.

What's happening to me? Finn thought. *I feel different. This is – fantastic!*

And then, with the greatest joy he had ever

known, he stopped wondering about what was happening, and gave himself up to the sea. He felt as if he had come home. He began to twist about in the water, feeling it wash through his hair and along the length of his body. Then he began to move his arms and legs as he'd seen swimmers do on the TV. He could swim! He was swimming! It was as easy as breathing, easier even than walking on land!

There was only one thing that spoilt the loveliness of being in the water, and that was the growling, thrumming noise of the *Janine*'s engine. He wanted to get beyond it and listen to the sea.

He began to glide through the water, his arms and legs moving automatically, going fast and straight. His eyes drank in every new and wonderful sight: the play of sunlight through the current, the distant outline of a submerged rock, a slowly crawling starfish on the seabed below.

He had been underwater for a long while, holding his breath without thinking about it, but at last he felt the need to surface and suck in another lungful of air. Then he was down again, racing under the surface of the ocean, feeling as if he could swim on and on forever.

Now that the rumble of the boat's engine had

faded, he was in a whole new world of sounds. Below him he could hear the faint rattle of a pebble dislodged by a lobster as it climbed over a rock. Above, that muffled *Whee! Whee!* must be the call of a gull swooping low over the water. And the slow, rhythmic *thud, scrape* was the rumble of waves breaking on the beaches up the coast.

But now, through it all, came the most beautiful sound he'd ever heard. It was faint, hardly audible above the sucking and rippling of the water, but it was getting louder.

Someone, or something, was whistling.

There was a familiar note to the sound, something that touched him and drew him on. Before he could think about it any more, a shape appeared ahead, long and grey with flippers and a tail. It was a young dolphin.

He was seized with sudden panic.

It's as big as me, he thought. *I don't know about dolphins. What if it attacks me?*

The dolphin swam up alongside Finn and brushed against his back. Finn swerved nervously away, but the dolphin tapped him playfully with his snout. He began to make a kind of vibrating sound that thrummed in Finn's head.

I can understand you, he thought. *You want to be my friend!*

He needed to breathe again. He shot up to the surface and took a gulp of air. The dolphin surfaced too. With both their heads out of the water, they stared at each other.

He likes me! Finn thought with astonishment. *He wants to play!*

The dolphin dived down and began to swim away, but he was making the whistling sound again, as if he was inviting Finn to follow him. Finn was afraid that he wouldn't be able to keep up, but he found that he could swim easily, and twist, plunge and roll every bit as well and as fast as his new friend.

What was the dolphin doing now? He was clicking his beak, sending a signal of some kind.

It means 'leap'. He's going to leap! thought Finn. *Yes, there he goes!*

The dolphin was shooting up through the water, breaking the surface, flying through the air and diving down again. He twisted round, coming back to Finn, making the vibrating sound again. Finn felt the same lovely soft feeling as the buzzing set up an answering echo in his head.

It's what a kiss must feel like, he thought, and for a

moment he felt an old pain. His mother must have kissed him when he was a baby, but he couldn't remember her at all.

The dolphin seemed to be gathering himself for another leap. He was whistling and clicking to Finn.

He wants me to leap with him, thought Finn. *I don't think I – Oh –*

Yes, I can!
Whoosh!

He'd
done it!
He landed
back on
the water
too hard,
making
a bigger
splash
than his
friend, but
the leap
had felt
incredible,
powerful
and free.

He tried making the buzzing sound. It didn't come out right, but it wasn't a bad effort. The dolphin seemed to like it, anyway. He stroked Finn with his flipper, and bumped alongside him in a friendly way. Then, somehow, they both had the same idea at the same time. They dived a bit and powered up through the water, surfacing at the same time, soaring through the air, then plunging back into the water side by side.

It was the first time in his life that Finn had ever played with a friend.

He could have stayed forever leaping and splashing in the sea, but now the dolphin was off again, streaking through the water as if he was answering a call. Finn followed him for a few minutes, but the dolphin was going too fast. He was racing further and further out to sea.

I've come too far out, Finn thought, suddenly alarmed.

He wanted to go back to the land, to feel normal again, to make sure that he really wasn't dead and drowned after all.

With one supple twist, he turned and swam effortlessly towards the sound of the breaking waves. A few minutes later, he was standing on the beach, wringing the water out of his T-shirt and shorts. It was strange to be on land again. The wonderful power that had driven him through the sea had gone, and he was just awkward, clumsy Finn again.

He looked round fearfully, panic twisting his stomach. Charlie was probably still around somewhere. He might still be on the warpath.

He began to run up the hard sand and across the dunes that separated the beach from the coast road. He was going so fast that he had to double over for a little while to get rid of the stitch in his side. Then, slipping through the back streets of the village, avoiding the row of cottages facing the sea where Charlie, Amir and the Lambs lived, he made his way home, his head full of questions and his heart full of wonder.

It was quite a long walk back to the cottage on the cliff top. Once he was sure that he was out of range of Charlie and the other children, Finn's footsteps slowed to a crawl. There were so many thoughts buzzing around in his head that he hardly knew where to start.

'I always knew I was different,' he said out loud.

'But why? It's like I was two people: one in the sea, and one on land.'

A cow was looking at him over the gate leading into one of the fields that fanned out beyond the harbour and up into the hills beyond.

'What are you staring at?' he called out to her. 'So I'm talking to myself? I'm not a nutter, you know.'

But then he thought, *Perhaps that's it. Perhaps I am a nutter. Maybe there's something wrong in my head.*

He picked up a small branch that had fallen from a tree, bent and twisted by the sea wind, and started swishing at the nettles that fringed the path.

I've got to tell Dad what's happened. There's a sort of secret about me and he's got to know what it is. It must be why he's never let me go near water.

But the thought of telling his father that he'd been in the sea was frightening. Staying away from deep water was the most important rule. It had been drummed into Finn ever since he could remember.

I've just got to do it, he told himself sternly. *I've got to know what — who I am, and he's the only one who can tell me. But how am I going to start?*

He needn't have bothered trying to work it out, because when he reached the gate leading up the weed-choked path to the cottage door, Mr McFee was waiting for him, his arms crossed and his forehead scored with a deep scowl. He caught Finn painfully by the arm and yanked him inside.

'I saw you! I *saw* you! Down on the beach! I've told you a hundred times. What have I told you?'

'Not to go near the sea. But Dad—'

'And what did you do?'

'I was on the beach, but listen, Dad—'

'You disobeyed me. I'm not having it, Finn. I'm not. There'll be no supper for you tonight. You'll do what you're told from now on. And – and I'll take my slipper to you, so I will.'

'*Dad!*' said Finn desperately. 'Listen! I've got to talk to you! Something's happened to me. I didn't disobey you, honestly I didn't. I didn't mean to fall into the sea. Charlie Munro chased me down to the harbour and off the wall. I went in by accident. But, Dad, it was so – so amazing! I could swim! I could hear things! I made a friend, a dolphin . . . What is it about me, Dad? I know I'm different. You've got to tell me, please!'

Mr McFee's arm froze in mid-air.

'What are you talking about? There's nothing different about you. You're my son, aren't you? What do you mean, you could swim and hear things and met a . . . a . . . ? You're telling stories, you wee liar.'

'I swam, Dad. Far and fast and deep.' Finn's words were boiling out of him. 'It felt amazing in the water. I could see and hear in a different way, and there was a sort of change as soon as I was out of my depth. I only had to move my arms and legs and then I was swimming and I could stay for ages under the water without breathing. And the sounds! I could hear the most amazing things. And I met a dolphin. He was – I think he became my friend. I know it sounds incredible, but I could almost understand him! Dad, you've *got* to believe me.'

Mr McFee groaned, felt for his armchair and slumped down into it with a thump. It creaked alarmingly. He dropped his head into his hands.

'I knew this would happen one day,' he wailed. 'I knew you'd find out, and go off into the sea, and leave me just like she did.'

'Find out what? Who's "she"?' Finn's skin was prickling all over. 'What are you saying, Dad? You mean my – my mother?'

'Aye, son. Your mother. You didn't think I'd believe you? Well, you'll have a hard time believing me when I tell you the truth of it. You'd better sit down. And there's no need to look at me like that – like a scared wee rabbit. You've asked for the truth, and I'm going to tell it to you.' He pointed a shaking finger at one of the rickety chairs pulled up to the table, and Finn sat down on the edge of it, his eyes fixed nervously on his father's face.

For a long time, Mr McFee didn't speak. Then he levered himself up out of his chair.

'I need a cup of tea,' he grunted. 'You look like you do too. Wait here.'

He went into the tiny, cluttered kitchen, and Finn, who was sitting screwed up in desperate impatience, heard the running water and the clatter of mugs.

After what seemed like an age, his father came back, handed Finn a steaming mug and sat down.

'Right, son. Here it comes. The truth. I told you, you'll have a hard time believing it.' He stopped, and cleared his throat. 'She – your mother – was a selkie. Oh aye, you might well stare. She came from the sea. Most selkies are seal people, but there are dolphin people too. My Sylvie was one of them.'

Finn was shuddering with excitement. He was listening with all his attention, but what his father was telling him was so incredible that he could hardly take it in. He didn't dare to move in case his dad stopped talking, but Mr McFee wasn't looking at him. He was staring unseeingly at the dirt-encrusted window.

'Folks thought those old stories were just fairy tales told by grannies,' he went on. 'I did and all, until she walked out of the sea one night and stood there, begging me to go on singing, looking so beautiful—'

A light flashed in Finn's head.

'But that's in the poem! It's like the poem!' he interrupted. He thrust his hand into his pocket and pulled out the crumpled sheet of homework. It was still wet. Carefully, trying not to tear it, he opened it out. The writing was blurred, but he could still just read it. His eye ran down it, frantically trying to absorb the meaning.

'*She bore a child, a little boy*,' he read wonderingly. '*And her heart was filled with love.*' His throat suddenly felt tight. 'That's me, isn't it, Dad? Is that right? Did she love me like the poem says?'

'Oh aye, she loved you, right enough,' said Mr McFee, but Finn had bent his head back to the poem and didn't notice the tears that were trickling down his father's cheeks.

'*O I am a woman on the land,*' he read. '*And a dolphin*

in the sea. That's like me, too! That's how I felt. Only I didn't become a dolphin; I was still a boy. I could just – sort of – feel like one.' He was reading on, his hands trembling with excitement as they clutched the paper. '*A miraculous child, a magical child, Is the son that is born to me.*'

He stopped and looked down at his father. Understanding flooded through him.

'You thought I was one too, didn't you?' he said. 'You thought I was a – a dolphin person? But I didn't *become* a dolphin. I think I might be a sort of half one, or something.'

Mr McFee took a deep, shuddering breath.

'Aye, I was afraid you were a selkie too. I've always dreaded it. I know that old poem. We had to learn it at school when I was a lad. I knew you were a – well, a magical boy, like it says. A different kind of boy, anyway. I thought if you went into the sea, you'd become like her, and swim away and leave me here on my own. Thought I could protect you, keep you safe on land.'

He put out his hand and grasped Finn's. For once, Finn didn't feel the urge to pull his away.

'You were an odd-looking wee thing. Beautiful, mind you, but your hands . . . "Why, look – they're almost like flippers," the midwife said. You grew into a normal-looking baby almost at once, but I suppose your mother knew something was different. I suppose I did too; I just didn't want to talk about it.'

'Why did she leave us? Leave *me*?' asked Finn, his voice coming out in a tight thread.

'She didn't mean to, son. Like I said, she loved you more than anything. She'd hover over you, sing to you, dance you around and make you laugh. But she'd get the urge to go out to sea every now and then, when her people came into the shore and called to her. She always came back, a bit quiet for a day or two afterwards, but happy enough.'

'But then . . . ?' prompted Finn.

His father heaved a shuddering sigh.

'You know what they all say about me? That I killed her? Well, they were right. Not in the way they think, but the boat I was working on killed her. One night she put you to bed in the normal way, and I was still out fishing. She must have heard her people calling and gone out to them. We were all so busy with the catch, we didn't see the dolphins. One of the lads caught her in his net. I tried and tried, but I couldn't free her.'

'It might not have been her!' Finn said eagerly. 'How can you be sure? She might still be out there. I could go and find her, Dad. I could bring her back.'

Mr McFee shook his head.

'It was her all right. When I'd got her out of the water at last, and she was lying on the deck in that horrible net, and the lads were busy in the stern bringing in the fish, she turned back into my Sylvie again. My lovely . . . Then her eyes began to cloud over. "Love Finn," she whispered. And she . . . When it was over, she turned back into a dolphin again, slowly. It was dark, a dark night, but I felt the change as I held her in my arms. No one else saw. I couldn't tell them. How could I? How could I ever tell anyone? Who would have believed me? The secret's burned me away inside ever since.'

'What did you do with – with her then?' Finn managed to say.

'I slid her body gently back into the sea and let her go. Then we brought the boat back into harbour, and I ran home, and there you were, sleeping in your cot as if nothing had happened. I never went out to sea again. I left the boat and the job and all the rest of it. They call me a murderer, and I never answer back because they're right in a sort of way. It was our nets that killed her, and I was a part of all that. It was because of us fishermen that she died.'

'Why didn't you tell me before, Dad?' whispered Finn.

'I couldn't. I was too scared you'd blame me for killing your mother. And I was scared you'd swim off out there and leave me.'

'I wanted to, just for a moment,' said Finn honestly. 'It felt so free and lovely in the water, and when I met the dolphin I could tell that he liked me. Ordinary kids don't like me. They never have. I suppose they can tell that I'm strange.'

'Folks don't like me much either,' replied his dad, 'but we've got each other, eh, son?'

His eyes were fixed on Finn with painful intensity, but Finn didn't notice. He had gone to the door and was looking out over the stretch of rough grass between the cottage and the cliff, which dropped away out of sight, down to the small rocky cove below. He felt a glow of happiness, a new kind of strength that he'd never known before.

It's as if I've found the half of me that was missing, he thought. *And now I know who I am. I'm not a selkie, but it was like being halfway there. A sea boy. Yes, that's* it. *I'm a sea boy.* A huge grin spread over his face. *Maybe it'll be different now that I know. Perhaps I can be a normal land boy too.*

He watched, without seeing, as a pair of swallows swooped and dived over the lane, catching insects in their tiny beaks.

'I need to go back into the sea,' he said. 'I've got to find out if – if it's real or not. I've got to *know.*' *And I want to find my dolphin friend again*, he thought. *Because if he's there, and he still likes me, I won't ever feel lonely again.*

Mr McFee started to protest, but then slowly, reluctantly, he nodded.

'You're not a wee boy any more, Finn, and I don't suppose I could stop you, even if I tried.'

Finn impulsively tugged at his arm.

'Come down the cliff path to the beach with me, Dad. If I know you're standing there, waiting for me on the shore, it'll feel more right, somehow.'

Mr McFee shuddered.

'Maybe, Finn. Maybe not. I'm not sure that I could bear to watch you, to be honest. Give me a bit of time, eh? Tomorrow maybe, when I've had the chance to get used to all this. It's too late this evening, anyway. The sun's going down fast.'

He got up out of his chair, put his hands on Finn's shoulders and looked into his son's face for a long moment.

'I've been a rotten dad to you,' he said at last. 'This thing – this secret – it's been eating me up inside. Holding me down, stopping me from doing everything I should have done. I ought to have told you about your mother years ago, but I thought that if you never found out, you'd stay safe.' He stopped and dropped his hands, then he smiled, and Finn, watching his face, thought he saw for the first time a glimpse of the man his father must once have been.

He squared his shoulders and pushed the ragged thatch of long hair out of his eyes.

'Things are going to change from now on, Finn,' he said, with a smile that reached his eyes. 'You'll see.'

Finn stared at him. His father looked different. Stronger. More confident.

'Sure, Dad,' he said, and stopped, afraid that if he said anything more the spell would be broken.

'So now,' said Mr McFee, walking briskly into the cottage's tiny kitchen, 'I'm going to cook us some supper.'

*

That evening was a golden one for Finn. While his dad cooked in the kitchen, Finn went out once again to stand by the broken cottage gate. The sun, setting behind the cottage, cast such a brilliant light over land and sea that everything seemed to glow with a deep radiance. In the warm air, bees fumbled around in the wild flowers that fringed the cliff top, and Finn could hear the sea birds quarrelling and fussing over their chicks, out of sight on their ledges on the cliff face below, where they had built their nests.

What's he – my friend – doing out there? he wondered. *Is he playing, like he did with me? I suppose he's got loads of other friends. Real ones. Dolphin ones.*

The thought made him feel a pang of jealousy.

The sun was sinking lower, and the shadow of the cottage was lengthening second by second. It was falling on Finn now, and the brilliant blue of the sea and sky was slowly darkening to a deep indigo.

What do dolphins do at night? he asked himself. *Do they sleep, like us?*

'Come and get your supper, son!' his dad called out at last. 'It's ready!'

Finn, suddenly starving, ran back into the cottage, then stopped at the door, his eyes wide with surprise. He and his dad had always eaten their meals

with their plates balanced on their knees in front of
the TV, but tonight Mr McFee had actually cleared
some of the clutter on the table, and set out proper
places. He'd fried up sausages and made chips too.

'This is great, Dad,' said Finn, sliding into his
chair.

He was too busy enjoying his supper to talk, and
it wasn't until he'd eaten the last bit of sausage, and
chased the last chip round his plate, that he realized
that his father hadn't said a word either.

Mr McFee had been eating more slowly than
Finn, and, looking up at him, Finn could see that
although the heavy, sad look had gone from his face,
his father's forehead was creased in a frown.

'That was great, Dad. Thank you very much,'
Finn said, hoping to cheer his father up.

Mr McFee nodded absently, but his thoughts were
elsewhere. Finn felt a stab of anxiety.

'You're not annoyed with me, are you, Dad?'

His father looked up in surprise.

'Annoyed? No, why would I be?' He sighed. 'It's
just that I really, really wish she was here. I don't
know how to help you with all this business. I can't
guide you like she'd have been able to do. There's
bound to be dangers out there in the sea. I should

know; I was a fisherman for years and years. But where you'll go and what you'll do – you'll be on your own, Finn, and it scares me.'

Finn laughed with relief.

'But I won't be alone, Dad. I'll have my friend to help me. The first thing I'll do is look for him, and I'll find him again. I know I will. You'll have to trust me, Dad. I'm going to be careful, but I'm going to be myself at last. I'm going to be her son as well as yours.'

An enormous yawn suddenly threatened to split his face in two. He was so tired that his bones felt as if they'd melt.

His father smiled at last.

'Get away to your bed, Finn. It's been quite a day, eh?'

Finn smiled back at him, then he climbed the steep, narrow steps to his little bedroom under the eaves, feeling stronger and happier than he had ever felt in his life.

'I'll see you in the morning, friend,' he whispered to himself as he climbed into bed.

A moment later, he was asleep.

Chapter Five

By a quarter past ten on the following morning, Amir, Charlie, Kyla and Dougie had all arrived at the lighthouse and were clustered round the kitchen table helping themselves to the plate of biscuits that Jas had put out. They looked up as Professor Jamieson put his head round the door.

'Hello, everyone,' he said, peering at them. 'Have you all come for lunch? I don't think we've got enough to go round.'

'It's OK, Dad,' said Jas. 'We're just having a meeting.'

Professor Jamieson knew all about meetings. He was always having them with colleagues who came to visit him.

'Good, good,' he said vaguely. 'Have you seen

my glasses, Jas? I can't find them anywhere.'

'They're in your pocket,' Jas said. 'I can see them sticking out.'

'Goodness me. So they are,' said the professor, pulling out his glasses and settling them on his nose. 'Well, I'll let you get on with it.' And he ambled out of the room.

'Right,' Jas said firmly. 'Let's go up to the lantern room. Dougie, you bring the biscuits.'

The lantern room was at the very top of the lighthouse tower. To get to it, the children had to go up a spiral staircase that got narrower and narrower, and then climb an iron ladder. They came up through a metal trapdoor set into the floor of the small round room.

In the old days, the lighthouse's lantern had been in this room. Originally lit by oil, and later by electricity, its sparkling mirrors had turned all day and all night on a pool of silvery mercury, sending a beam of brilliant light far out to sea to warn sailors to steer clear of the rocks. The lamp, the mirrors, the mercury and all the complicated old machinery had gone now. The lantern room was just a small, round, empty space with clear glass walls on all sides.

This was Jas's special place. She had brought up a

stack of cushions so she could lie down comfortably on the hard metal floor. She kept a little stock of her favourite books here too, a photograph of her mother, who had died when she was five, and a box of her own secret treasures.

You could see for miles in all directions from the lantern room. The view to the front was over the harbour and far out across the sea. To the back, was the village of Stromhead and the hills behind it, and on each side the beaches and cliffs stretched away along the coast.

In the lantern room, Jas felt like a bird, looking down from on high over the world below.

Amir and Kyla often came up here with her. Amir liked to sit cross-legged with his laptop on his knee, doing complicated internet searches, while Kyla drew pictures and borrowed Jas's crayons to colour them in, and Jas sat against one of the glass walls reading a book. None of the three usually talked much. They just liked the feeling of doing their own thing in each other's company.

Jas didn't often invite Charlie to the lantern room. He was too energetic and restless to be comfortable in a small space. He would stand at the side of the tiny room that overlooked the sea for a few minutes, squinting up at the cloud formations and critically watching the surface of the water to gauge the weather and the chances of a good catch if he took out his little boat to fish; then he'd dash back down the steep stairs, his boots clanging on the metal treads all the way to the bottom.

Only Dougie had never been in the lantern room.

'You're not old enough,' Kyla had always told him crushingly. She was proud of her friendship with Jas and Amir, and didn't want Dougie muscling in. 'Us older ones, we're the Lighthouse Crew. You have to be ten to be one of us.'

Dougie was so excited at being admitted at last to

Jas's special place that he was unusually quiet as he followed Kyla upstairs, and his mouth opened in a large silent O when he came up into the small bright space and took in the astonishing view on all sides through the glass walls. Then he squeezed himself into the little corner between Amir and Jas and started fiddling with his chain and padlock.

There wasn't much space in the lantern room once everyone was inside. Jas let down the trapdoor and gave each of them a cushion to sit on. For a long moment, no one said anything.

'I love it up here,' Amir said at last. 'You feel sort of free. As if you were flying. You are lucky, Jas.'

'I know. It's amazing,' said Kyla. 'Why don't you decorate it a bit more? I've got a really sweet garland of paper flowers. They'd look gorgeous strung up from the ceiling.'

'That's so − that's just ridiculous,' growled Charlie. 'This is a lighthouse, Kyla, not a stupid . . .'

He stopped, looking guilty. He'd promised himself to be nice to everyone for evermore and never lose his temper again.

'I wish you wouldn't lean against the glass like that, Amir,' Kyla said anxiously. 'What if it's not very strong and you fall right through it? It's a really long way down. You'd break all your bones and be cut all over with broken glass.'

'Don't be silly, Kyla,' Jas said sternly. 'It's quite safe up here. You've got a mind like a disaster movie.'

'Yes, but . . .' began Kyla, but at that point a seagull perched on the roof overhead, and the scratching of its feet distracted everyone.

Dougie nudged Amir to get his attention.

'I wish the old lantern was still here,' he whispered to Amir. 'I'd like to know how it worked.'

'I'll find you a picture of one on the internet,' said Amir kindly. 'There's loads of different kinds of lighthouses. I looked them up.'

Dougie beamed at him gratefully.

'I'm one of you now, aren't I?' he said. 'I'm in the Lighthouse Crew.'

Jas cleared her throat loudly, calling the meeting to order.

'Well,' she began. 'You know why we're here. We've got to decide what to do about Finn. We've got to – I don't know – be nicer to him, or something.'

'I know,' said Amir, 'but you must admit that he's a bit, well, creepy.'

'He's got a nice face,' said Kyla, her head on one side as she thought about Finn, 'but the way he sort of sneaks around all the time, it's a bit . . .'

'Creepy,' finished Amir.

Jas frowned.

'Yes, but even if he is, well, creepy, we shouldn't be so horrible to him. We always have been.'

'And yesterday we might have actually killed him,' put in Kyla.

'Not you,' Charlie said, biting his lip. 'It was all my fault that he fell into the sea. I was the one who chased him. Something sort of got into me. You know what I'm like when I lose my temper.'

Nobody said anything.

'Have you seen his house?' Kyla said at last. 'It's awful. All broken down and dark. I'm glad I don't have to live there. And his horrible dad. You know what they say about him?'

No one said anything. They had all heard the rumours.

'To be fair on us,' said Amir, 'Finn does smell a bit. His clothes are really old and dirty.'

'They're too small for him, too,' said Dougie, whose voice was getting louder as his confidence rose.

'That's not his fault,' objected Jas. 'He hasn't

got anyone to look after him.'

'I know I was out of order chasing him,' said Charlie, 'but you've got to admit he's weird. There's something about him. Something . . . different.'

'But we still shouldn't be mean to him,' said Jas. 'I mean, everyone's weird, if you think about it.'

'I'm not,' said Dougie indignantly.

'Yes you are,' said Charlie. 'You're eight.'

'Eight's not weird!'

'It is when you're eleven,' said Jas. 'Anyway, look at *me*. My mum was African. People round here think that's really odd.'

'And I'm Pakistani,' said Amir.

'You're right, Jas. But I've got a horrible temper,' said Charlie. 'That's *bad* weird, not just weird.'

'I don't think I'm weird at all,' said Kyla, although she kept a careful eye on Jas as she spoke.

Everyone looked at her. Kyla bit her lip, pretending not to be anxious.

'You know what?' Jas said, laughing. 'I don't think you are!'

Kyla looked sideways, examining her reflection in the glass wall beside her. Then she turned back, satisfied, before a horrible idea hit her.

'But if I'm the only one who's not weird, doesn't

that make me, well, weird?' she said.

'Never mind about you!' Charlie burst out impatiently. 'I know what I've got to do. I've got to go and find Finn and say sorry.'

'It's not just you, Charlie,' said Amir. 'I felt awful when he fell into the sea. It made me realize how mean we've been, not letting him do stuff with us, ignoring him all the time . . .'

'I've just thought of something terrible,' said Kyla. 'We don't actually know for certain that he got out of the sea, do we? Amir might have missed him when he went down to look. None of us actually saw him. He might have, I don't know, rolled further into the harbour, under one of those big boats. He might have got all tangled up in the propeller. He might have been chopped into bits.'

The others looked at her, their mouths open with shock. For once, Kyla's fears seemed horribly possible.

'We didn't think of that, did we,' whispered Jas. 'We should have told a grown-up. Raised the alarm or something.'

At that moment, a muffled thump came up through the floor.

'What's that?' yelped Dougie.

'It's the outside door,' said Jas. 'Someone's shut it.'

'They've locked us in!' said Kyla. 'We can't get out! We'll be here all night!'

'Shh!' said Jas. 'Listen.'

They all listened. There were footsteps on the stairs, climbing fast, higher and higher, nearer and nearer to the lantern room.

'It's Finn's ghost!' shrieked Kyla. 'He's come to haunt us! We'll never get out of here alive!'

Chapter Six

It was late when Finn woke that morning. He lay staring up at the familiar pattern of peeling paint on the ceiling above his bed wondering why he was feeling so different. Then the memory of everything that had happened the day before flooded back into his mind.

It can't have been true! he thought. *I must have dreamed it all! Me, swimming? Far out at sea — making friends with a dolphin? I must be going crazy!*

He leaped out of bed, dragged on his clothes, and jumped two at a time down the narrow stairs into the sitting room below. Where was his father? The chair by the window, where he usually sat for most of the day, was empty, and outside Finn could hear the sound of chopping.

He wrenched open the cottage door and ran outside.

Mr McFee, an axe in his hand, was hacking away at a dead tree, which had fallen over in last winter's gale and had been left to lie at the end of the jungle that had once been a garden. He looked up when he heard the door open.

'So you've woken up at last!' he called out. 'I thought you'd sleep all day. Get yourself some breakfast and—'

'Did it really happen, Dad?' Finn interrupted. 'Did I dream it all? Am I really . . . ?'

'Oh aye,' replied his father 'It happened all right. You're a magical boy, and I'm trying to get my head round it too.'

'And can I go down there, into the sea, Dad? You said I could. You said—'

'I can't stop you, can I?' his father answered. 'But get some food inside you first, Finn. You'll be needing all the energy you can get.'

Half an hour later, Finn had bolted his breakfast and was making his way carefully down the steep path that led from the cliff top to the narrow beach below. He looked round wonderingly. He'd lived right on top of this little cove all his life, but that morning it looked to him as strange and wonderful as a foreign country.

The tiny bay was a perfect, private place. The strip of golden sand, hemmed in on both sides by steep rocks, was quite hidden. Only a boat passing close along the shore could see into it, and judging by the overgrown state of the footpath that scored a deep scar up the face of the cliff, few people ever bothered to clamber down to it.

But when Finn crossed the beach and was standing at last at the edge of the water, he felt a kick of nerves in his stomach, and his heart started to beat uncomfortably fast.

What if I imagined everything after all? he thought. *Or even if I didn't, maybe the magic only works once!*

He looked doubtfully down into the water. The little waves, soft and shining under the bright morning light, rolled and lapped innocently on the sand, seeming to invite him in. Finn took a deep breath, kicked off his shoes, and took a first tentative step into the water. He stopped, waiting for the change, waiting for that powerful, joyous feeling to surge back and welcome him into the sea.

Nothing happened. The water felt cold, and his

arms and legs sprouted goose bumps. He almost wanted to run out of the water and race back up to the safety of the cottage, but then, turning to look back, he caught sight of a figure standing at the edge of the cliff above, watching him. It was his father.

He'll think I was making everything up. He'll think I was just telling a story, he told himself. *He'll think I'm a coward.*

He breathed in deeply, took a few more steps, then flopped forward, letting his feet leave the safety of the sand beneath the water.

And there it was! That warmth and certainty again! The water seemed to welcome him, as it had done before. He swam slowly forward, letting his ears tune into the sounds of the ocean, and feasting his eyes on the shifting patterns of light that the rising sun was striking through the water. He came up for air at last, and rolled on to his back. He could see his father, still there, standing at the top of the cliff.

Finn raised his hand and waved and watched his father turn away, then, his confidence soaring, he dived again and shot out to sea, away from the shrill squawks of the nesting seabirds and the beat of the waves breaking against the rocks that fringed the beach. He couldn't wait to get into the quietness of the deep water, where he might pick up the whistles of the dolphins, his brothers and sisters, his friends.

He didn't know how long it was before he heard them, but there at last was the beautiful, piercing sound – the best kind of music that Finn had ever heard.

But what was *that*? The whistling sound was confused, and now that he was coming closer he could tell that there wasn't one tune in the dolphin music, but many of them. They sounded frantic, too; excited but frightened at the same time. Finn had been swimming fast, but now he slowed, feeling suddenly shy. He hadn't expected to meet a whole group of dolphins. He had only wanted to find his friend. What if the others didn't like him? What if they were angry and unfriendly, like Charlie was on land? They might turn on him.

It was too late to go back. A long grey shape was already streaking towards him, whistling in a familiar way. Finn knew who it was at once. It was his friend! And now he was being nudged and encouraged forward towards the group that he could see ahead, a boiling mass of grey bodies, cavorting and twisting in the water. A few minutes later, he had reached them, and then he was right among them, treading water in the middle of the pod. To his relief, none of them seemed to notice him. They were too busy and excited, though one touched him gently with her nose as if in welcome before plunging away towards the others. He tried to count them. Were there five? Six? Seven? They were moving about so fast, it was impossible to tell.

Perhaps they're my family! he thought, with a sudden flash of excitement. *They might be my cousins, or my aunties and uncles!*

The thought gave him confidence and he began to move from one dolphin to another, touching them to introduce himself. He could feel their welcome and their friendliness. But he could see that they were distracted too. They kept shooting up to the surface of the sea, where bright things were bobbing about on the surface of the water.

Something floated just above Finn's head. It was round and a dazzling orange colour.

A jellyfish! thought Finn. *I hope it doesn't sting. No — it's a balloon!*

A string was hanging down from the balloon, with a soggy scrap of paper tied to the end.

It's the balloons from Dougie's party, thought Finn. *They've blown right out to sea.*

A dolphin was nudging him aside, trying to grab the balloon. It bobbed away from her first attempt. The dolphin flipped over on to her back and grasped the balloon in her mouth.

She thinks it's a jellyfish too! She's eaten it!

For a moment he thought it was funny, and then he saw that the balloon's string was caught in the dolphin's teeth.

She was twisting herself round to get rid of it, but only succeeded in tangling it over one of her flippers.

She began to whistle in distress. The more she tried to free herself, the tighter the string bit into her. It was cutting her flipper where it joined her body. Finn swam up to her. He seemed to know instinctively how to soothe her, nudging and stroking her. He tried to slip the string off her flipper, but the dolphin wouldn't keep still. She kept straining against him while the string knotted itself round her tighter and tighter. Working furiously, Finn managed to release her at last, but she swam straight back towards the next balloon, a big yellow one, and began to plunge up through the water to catch it. All around Finn, the other dolphins were snatching at the balloons too, trying to eat them and getting tangled in the strings.

How can I stop them? Finn thought desperately.

He began to swim about frantically, grabbing the strings of as many balloons as he could see, but the dolphins were splashing around so busily, nudging and shoving as they tried to eat the balloons, that he couldn't get hold of more than a couple.

I've got to save them! he told himself. *But I can't do it on my own. I need help!*

He lifted his head high out of the water and looked around. There, in the distance, was land. He could see the harbour, with the boats bobbing about on the swell, the cluster of houses behind it, and the lighthouse higher up. Further along, where the cliffs rose from the town, was the little cove below his home.

Dad! I'll go and fetch Dad! he thought. *No — he won't know what to do. He hasn't got a boat or anything.*

He was treading water in an agony of indecision when the answer suddenly came to him. Before he had even thought it through, he took off and began to power through the water towards the harbour and the beach that lay beyond it. He would fetch Jas's dad. Professor Jamieson was a marine biologist. He knew everything about the sea and the animals in it. He would know what to do.

In an incredibly short time, he was standing on the beach. He shook the wet hair out of his eyes and ran across the sand in his bare feet as fast he could, wishing with all his heart that the power he felt in the water worked on land too. But he was just awkward, clumsy Finn again.

He scrambled over the sand dunes at the head of the beach and set off up the steep, narrow road that led to the lighthouse. He was nearly there when a movement in the lantern room, high above, caught his eye.

Jas is up there! he thought. *And that looks like Amir.*

And Charlie and . . . they're all there together.

Before the familiar sense of loneliness could sap his confidence, he was at the lighthouse door. He had lifted his hand to ring the doorbell when he saw a note that was stuck to the door with a drawing pin:

Back at 11. Please leave the delivery by the back door.
D. Jamieson.

'No!' he shouted out loud. 'You've got to be at home! You have to help! You must!'

The thought of the dolphins tangling themselves in string, risking maiming and drowning to eat those horrible balloons, made him throw all caution aside.

'I'll have to go up there and tell Jas,' he said. 'Maybe she'll know what to do.'

And before he could give himself time to dread seeing them all, especially Charlie, who might still be in a murderous rage, he pushed open the door, letting it bang shut behind him, and began to climb the steep wrought-iron stairs to the lantern room, ignoring the clang of the metal treads under his pounding feet.

He reached the top at last, thrust the trapdoor up, and burst into the tiny glass room with the force of a cork shooting out of a champagne bottle.

'Help! You've got to come and help!' he said.

He stopped, surprised at himself. He'd never spoken like that to the others before. He'd never dared. By the looks on their faces, he could see that he'd astonished them too. He took a deep breath. He couldn't begin to explain to them the strange power that had transformed him in the sea. He only knew that somehow he had to persuade them to help him free the dolphins.

They were all staring at him, mouths hanging open.

Finn frowned. It almost looked as if they were afraid of him. What was wrong with them all? Did he look different from the old Finn? Did he actually look scary? Would they hate him even more?

Jas was the first to recover.

'Finn!' she whispered. 'Is it really you? We thought . . .'

'We thought you might be dead,' groaned Charlie. 'We thought I'd killed you.'

'Are you dead?' asked Dougie. 'Are you a ghost?'

The image of the dolphin tied up in string came rushing back to Finn, and a bolt of urgent impatience shot through him.

'Of course I'm not dead,' he said indignantly. Then he hesitated. His mind seemed to be working at top speed, and he'd suddenly realized how to go on. 'I'm not dead,' he went on more calmly, 'but it's no thanks to you. My head missed one of those wee launches by inches. If it had knocked me out . . .'

'I did try to find you, Finn,' said Amir anxiously. 'I jumped into the water and looked everywhere. You'd . . . disappeared. We knew you couldn't have drowned, because the water was so shallow. We thought you'd gone round to the beach.'

'Are you *sure* you're not a ghost?' asked Dougie, sounding almost disappointed.

Finn ignored him. 'The point is,' he went on, 'you owe me one – especially you, Charlie.'

Charlie made a sort of gurgling noise and nodded guiltily.

'We looked for you everywhere,' he said gruffly. 'All over the rocks. I wanted to say sorry, Finn. I really did.'

'And you, Dougie.' Finn turned to glare at the little boy. 'You didn't invite me to your party. You tore up my invitation.'

'How did you kn—?' began Dougie, then stopped

as a blush spread up his face.

'So now,' Finn swept on, 'it's payback time. You've got to help me. There's something I really, really need you to do.'

The five children had been staring at him, fascinated, almost unable to recognize in this new, confident, powerful boy the old Finn that they'd shunned all their lives.

Jas cleared her throat.

'As a matter of fact,' she said, 'it's really nice to . . . I'm glad you've come here, actually. I should have invited you up to the lantern room ages ago. We all feel bad about the way we've treated you, and we came up here to think about how we could . . . could do something to show we're sorry. We – well – we're the Lighthouse Crew, you see, and we want you to be in it too.'

Finn stared at her for a moment. What was she talking about? A crew? He couldn't take it in. He latched on to the bit about them being sorry. What she was saying was so surprising that he could hardly believe it. But she had given him his chance, and he took it.

'I'll tell you exactly how to show you're sorry,' he said. 'There's something you've got to do for me *now*. Only it's not really for me; it's for the dolphins.'

'The what?' said Kyla.

'Dolphins?' said Amir.

'Why dolphins?' said Dougie. 'Wouldn't you rather have a ride on my new bike?'

'Are you talking about the pod that's been out in the bay for the past few weeks?' said Charlie. 'My dad's been telling me about them. Great jumpers they are, leaping about as if—'

'Those dolphins, yes,' said Finn. 'They're fantastic, beautiful, there's one who . . .' He stopped himself. There was no time to explain anything, and he wasn't sure if he even wanted to. 'They're in trouble, the dolphins are, I mean. You've got to help me get out there and sort it out. They're going to die if—'

'What sort of trouble, Finn?' said Jas, frowning at him. 'And how do you know?'

'Never mind how I know,' snapped Finn. 'It's the balloons, the ones from Dougie's party. They've landed out at sea and the dolphins think they're jellyfish. They keep trying to eat them. The strings have got tangled in their flippers and are hurting them. It's horrible! Please, don't just sit there! You've got to come and *help*!'

No one said anything. They were looking at him, stunned. Amir cleared his throat.

'I've read about plastic bags and bottles and stuff in the sea choking animals, but this thing with balloons sounds kind of crazy. I mean, they're not made of plastic, are they? I thought they were made of rubber or something.'

'It's not crazy! It's happening now! Please, you've got to help me!' Finn balled his fists and shook them in frustration.

'How do you know about it anyway? About what the dolphins are doing?' asked Jas. 'Did someone tell you? You couldn't have gone out into the bay without a boat.'

'You've sort of changed,' said Dougie. 'You don't look the same any more.'

'You've grown or something,' said Charlie. 'You look taller.'

'How did you hide from us all?' asked Kyla. 'We looked for you everywhere.'

'There's no time to explain!' snapped Finn. 'I'll tell you everything later, but we've got to get out there *now*, and fetch those stupid balloons back in.'

'They're not stupid balloons. They're from my . . .' Dougie stopped as it occurred to him that it might be tactless to mention his party in front of Finn.

'I don't see what we can do, anyway,' said Charlie. 'The whole thing's daft. I'm not saying you're wrong about the dolphins eating them, mind, but even if we went out to sea, we'd never find a bunch of balloons. The sea's an awful big place.'

'We'd need a boat, anyway,' said Jas.

'That shouldn't be a problem.' Amir's eyes behind his glasses were gleaming with fascination as he stared at Finn, like he was an interesting form of wildlife. 'Charlie's got a boat.'

Charlie's chest swelled. His father had bought a new dinghy for the *Janine* and he'd given Charlie his old one. The *Peggy Sue* was Charlie's pride and joy. Mr Munro had taught him how to row and sail, and Charlie was allowed to go out in her on calm days, as long as he wore a life jacket and took Amir with him to crew.

'Where is it?' said Finn urgently. He'd forgotten that Charlie had a boat.

'What?'

'Your boat!'

'She's pulled up on the beach. Oh, you mean . . .'

'Yes, I do mean.' Finn nodded vigorously. 'I'll help you launch her.'

'Well, I don't know,' said Charlie. 'You don't have a clue about boats. I'm not being mean, but you're hopeless at doing stuff, Finn. You know you are. Anyway, it's like I told you. You'd never find a few balloons out there in the bay. It's just too big.'

Finn took a step forward. The space in the lantern room was so tiny that Kyla had to pull back her knees. He pointed a finger into Charlie's face.

'Payback time, remember? You could have killed me. I was terrified.'

He couldn't believe what he was doing. He'd never before dared stand up to Charlie. Charlie reared backwards, away from Finn's finger, looking scared, a flush of shame creeping up his neck.

'I know. I told you I'm sorry. I was out of order. I'm not saying I believe in all that stuff about the balloons or anything, but I don't mind taking you out in the boat if that's what you want. Like you say, I owe you one. You'll love the *Peggy Sue*, Finn. She's a grand wee—'

'Well, come on then,' said Finn, turning towards the stairwell. 'Let's go.'

'Hold on a minute!' Charlie was getting up with maddening slowness. 'You can't just jump in a boat and go. We have to fetch the oars and the sail and the life jackets and everything.'

'Where are they?' demanded Finn.

'In the shed on the harbour. By the *Janine*'s berth.' His grin suddenly faded. 'I'm not supposed to take her out on my own, though, without permission from a . . .' He stopped, hunting for the word. 'A responsible adult.'

'Your dad's out lobstering,' said Finn. 'We can't wait for him to come back. He could be hours.'

'I'll come,' said Jas. 'I love sailing. There you are, Finn. You and I will go out in the boat with Charlie. We'll be the crew.'

'You're not leaving me out,' said Amir indignantly. 'I've sailed with Charlie loads of times. And I can do life-saving.'

'We don't need to worry about the "responsible adult" bit either,' said Jas. 'My dad's an adult. He doesn't know a thing about boats and sailing. If I ask him casually, he'll think it's all quite normal. He probably won't even hear me. He'll be too busy writing his paper on limpets.'

'He's not in,' said Finn. 'He left a note on the door. It's why I came up here.'

'Oh, he's in all right,' said Jas. 'He always does that when he doesn't want people to disturb him.'

Dougie had been wriggling uncomfortably on his cushion.

'I wish I could come, Finn, but I can't,' he said unhappily. 'I'd be late for my dinner, and Mum would go crazy. It's so unfair. Kyla stays out all the time, but Mum won't let me.'

Kyla was shaking her head.

'You're nuts, all of you,' she said. 'Go out to sea with Charlie in a little boat? What if a storm comes up? What if there's killer whales out there? They come in close to shore sometimes. My dad's seen them. You could all be knocked into the sea and . . .' She realized that no one was taking any notice. 'Well I'm not coming, anyway. It's far too risky,' she finished lamely.

'That's just as well,' Jas said crisply. 'We need you to stay here at HQ for back-up. Got your mobile with you?'

Kyla nodded.

'Good. You wait up here. We'll send you an SOS call if anything goes wrong. You can alert my father, or—'

'Or any responsible adult,' said Amir.

Charlie had pressed his face up against the glass wall and was looking out to sea.

'What do you mean, *If anything goes wrong?* I'm a good sailor, so I am. You can trust me. And like I said, it's great weather for a sail,' he said. 'We won't be seeing any dolphins, though. You never do when you're looking for them.'

'I told you. You can leave that bit to me,' said Finn, who had been dancing with impatience. 'Now come *on!* And, Jas, bring some scissors with you. We'll need them to cut the strings.'

'What strings?' said Jas.

'The strings tying up the dolphins! I told you!' Finn almost yelled.

'Oh yes, of course – the strings,' she said soothingly, and Finn could tell she was humouring him.

I don't care if they believe me or not, he thought. *As long as Charlie gets me out to sea. I'll show them!*

It seemed like an age to Finn before the *Peggy Sue* was ready to be launched off the beach. He ran off to the harbour with Charlie and Amir to fetch the kit for the boat, while Dougie headed off unhappily for home, and Jas went to find her father, leaving Kyla alone in the lantern room, sitting on a pile of cushions, finishing off her drawing.

'Dad,' said Jas, putting her head round the door of her father's study. 'I'm going out for a little sail with Charlie and Amir.'

She'd expected her father to say, 'Hmm? What was that, darling? Now come and look at this! I've just made an extraordinary discovery.'

But instead, Professor Jamieson gave her a sharp look over the rims of his glasses, which he was wearing, as usual, on the end of his nose.

'Sailing? With Charlie Munro? What's the wind like? Is his father going out with you?'

Jas put her hand in her pocket so that he wouldn't see her crossing her fingers.

'No, but Charlie's passed loads of proficiency tests, and Mr Munro lets him go out alone, and I've got my mobile, and Amir's coming, and we'll be wearing life jackets, and—'

'Well, don't go far,' said Professor Jamieson. 'I'll come down to the beach in a little while and watch out for you.'

Jas gently closed his study door, letting her breath out with relief, and dashed off to join the others at the harbour.

Finn had been watching out for her. He was afraid that someone would come and tell them not to go, or that Charlie would change his mind.

'Here, take these,' said Charlie, dumping a bundle of life jackets into his arms. 'Jas, you bring the oars. Amir and I will take the mast and sails.'

A few minutes later, they were on the beach, watching as Charlie methodically prepared the *Peggy Sue*, setting up the mast, and sorting out the ropes. Finn almost had to bite his tongue to stop himself begging Charlie to hurry. He didn't want to annoy him now.

But as he helped the others to shove the boat down the beach and launch her into the water, Finn felt anxious for a different reason. He would have to tell them what had happened when he'd fallen into the sea, and he didn't know how to begin.

He waited until the wind had caught the sail, and they were a good distance out from the beach. The little town of Stromhead, with its old stone harbour walls, its white painted cottages with their grey slate roofs, and the lighthouse pointing its white finger up to the sky, was rapidly shrinking as they scudded away across the rippling water.

'Happy now, Finn?' said Charlie. Then, speaking more gruffly, in the voice of a skipper, he barked out, 'Jas, move over here or she'll list to starboard.

Amir, ease the sail to pick up the wind. Go on,
Finn — where are we supposed to be going?'

Finn gulped.

'Listen,' he said desperately. 'There's no easy
way to say this, so here goes. You know that poem
we've got to learn for homework? The one about
the selkie?'

Charlie groaned.

'Haven't even read it yet. I hate poems.'

'I've read it. I love it,' said Jas. *A fisherman sat on
the lonely shore* . . . It's beautiful.'

Finn looked at her gratefully.

'Well, the thing is, the poem's true. It's about
my — my mother, and — and me. She was a selkie.
My mum, I mean. Only a dolphin one, not a seal.
And I'm the . . . Well, I know it sounds stupid . . .
but *I'm* the magical boy. When I fell into the sea, a
sort of power came over me. I could swim, really
fast, and hear everything through the water, and —
well — understand the dolphins. I felt like I was one
of them.'

Charlie let out a disbelieving grunt.

Amir laughed incredulously.

'It's a scientific impossibility, Finn. You're not
telling us you're serious? We're not idiots, you know.'

'I know you're not idiots,' said Finn. 'And I know how weird it sounds. But it's true. Didn't you wonder where I'd disappeared to when I fell into the harbour?'

'Yes,' said Jas slowly. She was frowning at him, trying to understand. 'The tide was out, and we thought you'd waded round the harbour wall and run out up the beach.'

'No. I – When the – the *change* came over me, I swam out to sea. I met this dolphin and he led me to the group.'

'Amir! Loosen the boom! I'm going to tack to port!' snapped

Charlie. 'Finn, stop telling us a silly fairy story. Where are we supposed to be going?'

'I'll show you. I'll hear them whistling, and I'll lead you to them. Just follow me.'

And under the horrified and astonished eyes of the others, he threw himself over the edge of the boat.

'Finn! No!' shrieked Jas. 'Amir, go in after him! He'll drown!'

'I don't think so,' said Amir, in a strange voice. 'Look.'

The three children peered over the side of the boat into the green water. All they could see of Finn was a pale shape shooting through the water away from them as fast as a fish.

'What's happened to him?' breathed Jas.

'He looks like . . . an Olympic athlete or something,' said Amir.

Charlie was busy with the rudder.

'What are you idiots talking about?' he grunted.

'Just look, Charlie,' said Jas.

Charlie looked over the side of the boat.

'Can't see anything. He's disappeared. Thought he said he could swim?'

'He can. He's just gone so far, he's out of sight,' said Amir. 'Hey, look – he's coming back!'

Finn's head emerged from the water.

'What are you waiting for?' he said angrily. 'Why aren't you following me?' He slapped a hand down on to the surface of the water in frustration. 'There's no time to lose! We've got to get further out. Follow me!'

He plunged under the surface of the water and began to surge through it, his body a silver streak tinged with the green of the sea.

For a moment, no one in the boat moved. Then Charlie said, 'That's odd. The wind's changed. It's right behind us now. I suppose we'd better follow him.'

Chapter Seven

When Finn jumped off the boat into the water, he plunged down deep, further than he'd expected, and for a long scary moment he was filled with panic. But almost immediately, the change began. There was that kindly, embracing feeling of the sea again, the same glorious sense of power, and the amazing sights and sounds of the underwater world.

He had already picked up the whistles of distress from his dolphin friends further out to sea and was desperate to reach them.

Surfacing, he looked back and was relieved to see the *Peggy Sue* sailing after him, foam creaming along her bow wave. He had to go much more slowly than he wanted to. The wind wasn't much more than a breeze, and the little boat could go at only half his speed. And all the time, way out ahead, the dolphins' agitated whistles were calling to him.

After what seemed an age, he heard Jas's excited shout, and he lifted his head out of the water.

'Look! Over there! Balloons!'

'I don't believe this.' That was Charlie's voice. 'Am I dreaming?'

'This is really . . . It's just all wrong. I've got goose bumps,' Amir said.

Finn was suddenly afraid that the dolphins would panic if the *Peggy Sue* came right up on top of them. He let out a few experimental whistles, not sure if he was doing it right, and felt a jolt of relief when he heard the answering whistle of his first dolphin friend.

Then, suddenly, he was with them, right there inside the pod. The young female with the string caught round her flipper was writhing feebly. It was clear that she was exhausted, nearly ready to give up the struggle. On the surface there were fewer balloons now, and a couple of dolphins had strings hanging out of their mouths from the balloons they'd swallowed. It was too late to do anything about them. A couple were still playing with the few balloons that hadn't deflated, tossing them up into the air with flicks of their beaks.

Finn turned back to the *Peggy Sue*, which was now only a few metres away from the dolphins.

'Slow her down,' he called out Charlie. 'Don't scare them.'

There were rattling, creaking sounds as Amir released the jib to let the wind out of the sail, and the *Peggy Sue* glided to a halt.

Finn darted back into the mass of dolphins. His first friend came up to him, with clicks of greeting. Finn briefly buzzed him in reply, then made straight for the female tangled in the string. He moved alongside her, stroked his hand along her flank, and buzzed in what he hoped was a friendly and reassuring way. Then, moving gently, he began to nudge her towards the boat.

She was so tired that she could barely swim, and had only enough energy to come to the surface and breathe. She let Finn push her the last few metres until the two of them were right alongside the dinghy.

Jas was watching for him. He heard her take in a sharp breath as she saw the state the dolphin was in.

'Amir! Look at this!' she called out.

'I don't believe it! Finn was right!' he heard Amir say.

'I'll try to hold her,' Finn called up to them. 'Cut the string with your scissors.'

The dinghy rocked as Jas shifted her weight to pull out her bag from under the seat and fish out her scissors. She leaned as far as she could over the side to reach down to the tangled dolphin, with Amir beside her.

'Amir!' barked Charlie. 'Don't lean out like that, or we'll capsize. What are you doing, Jas?'

'I can't . . . reach,' panted Jas, straining forward with the scissors in her hand. 'It won't keep still. I'm scared of jabbing it with the scissors.'

'Hold on,' said Finn. 'I'll try to raise her up.'

He dived deeper, and, taking the young dolphin in his arms, he gently raised her whole body until she was half out of the water, treading water to keep himself afloat.

'That's it. Nearly! Yes, I've cut one bit. Tilt it over a bit, Finn. There – got it! That's its flipper freed. Wait, there's more string tying up its mouth.'

It was trickier cutting the string around the dolphin's mouth. Finn whistled and buzzed, stroking her as gently as he could, but she kept jerking

nervously away, and the dinghy lurched dangerously
as Jas lunged after the dolphin.

'You'll have to help me, Charlie,' Jas said. 'It
needs two of us.'

'I told you, we can't both hang over the side,' said
Charlie. 'We'll tip the boat over.'

'Not if I lean right out over
the other side,'
said Amir, 'like
they do in the
sailing races.'

'I don't
want to risk
it,' said
Charlie.
'This is *my*
boat. *I'm*
the skipper.
I—'

'Just
shut up,
Charlie,
and
look,
can't you?'

snarled Jas. 'This is an emergency. Do you *want* this poor creature to die?'

The dinghy rocked violently as Amir and Charlie moved. Then Charlie's head appeared alongside Jas's.

'That's terrible,' Charlie said, looking horrified. 'The poor thing. Here, Jas, pass me the scissors. I'm nearer its head than you are. Shift it round a bit this way, Finn. Can you catch its flipper and hold it steady? Why don't you sing a wee song? Aren't you supposed to sing to dolphins? To calm them down?'

'That's seals,' called out Amir, who was leaning so far out of the dinghy on the other side that he looked as if he was about to fall into the sea.

In spite of Finn's sea-strength, it was all he could do to keep the slippery dolphin from panicking completely and wriggling out of his arms.

'Hurry up, Charlie,' he said. 'I can't hold her much longer.'

'Nearly there,' said Charlie. He had the dolphin's head at the right angle now, and the scissors snipped away the string. 'There you are. It'll be all right now.'

As Jas and Charlie watched, with big grins on their faces, the dolphin shook herself, waggled her head, opened her beak experimentally, smacked her flippers down on the water, and with an energetic arching of her back, she was gone.

'High five!' yelled Charlie, slapping Jas's upraised hand. 'Life saved! That was great.'

'Hey, watch out!' shouted Amir. The dinghy had tipped alarmingly as Charlie and Jas stopped leaning over the side. 'You could have warned me you were moving. I nearly fell in.'

'What's Finn doing now?' said Jas. 'Look, he's grabbing the strings we cut. Wait, he's bringing them here to us!'

Of course I am, you idiot, thought Finn, not bothering to answer. *What do you want me to do? Leave all this junk in the sea so the others can get caught up in it too?*

He swam back to the dinghy and handed the strings and the last few balloons up to Jas. She leaned over the side and took them.

'I can't see any more,' he said. 'Can you?'

'No, but I'm sure we let loose a whole lot more.'

'You did,' Finn said grimly. 'The other dolphins have eaten the rest. Wait, there are a couple more over there.'

He streaked away again. The pod of dolphins was a little way away now, as the *Peggy Sue* had started drifting. Finn grabbed the last two balloons, swam back to the dinghy and handed them to Charlie and Amir. Finn could see awe and astonishment in the two boys' eyes as they took in the transformation that had come over him.

'This can't be happening,' said Amir, taking off his glasses to wipe off the sea water that was smearing them with salt. 'We've got to be in some kind of dream.'

'No one's ever going to believe us,' said Jas. 'Everyone's going to think we're crazy.'

'Better not say anything then,' retorted Charlie. 'Anyway, what's there to tell? Finn's an amazing swimmer, and we never knew it? Been keeping it secret all these years? You've got to admit, it's typical of him. All that selkie business, it's a load of rubbish. Of course it is.'

'Nobody can swim like that,' said Amir. 'Besides, how did he know about the balloons and where to find the dolphins?'

'Must have heard it from the crew of one of those launches that's been cruising around here.'

'What launches? And since when does Finn hang around talking to sailors?' said Amir.

Charlie didn't answer. His practical brain was

rebelling furiously against the idea of anything magical.

'We'll have to tell Kyla and Dougie,' said Jas.

'You can't trust Dougie to keep a secret,' Charlie scoffed. 'He'll blab it all out to his mum at once.'

'Yes, but I can hear what she'd say, can't you?' said Amir. '"What a sweet story, Dougie, darling. A boy who can swim like a fish? You're so cute, with your lovely imagination. Come here and give Mummy a kiss—"'

'Hey, look!' interrupted Charlie. 'Finn's in trouble now! One of the dolphins is attacking him!'

Finn heard.

'Shut up, idiot,' he called out. 'He's my friend. The first one I met. Watch this.'

He moved alongside his friend, buzzing. An answering buzz came. Then, just as they had done before, the pair of them dived a bit, and launched themselves upward, with perfect timing, in a glorious leap.

'Wow! That's amazing!' Finn heard the children cry out, but he and his friend were off again, diving and leaping, as they circled round the dinghy in a brilliant display of dolphin and sea-boy acrobatics.

Then, suddenly, his friend was off, streaking away

through the water in pursuit of his pod. Finn almost followed him, his whole body twitching with longing as he felt the call of the dolphins' distant whistles and the pull of friendship and freedom in the deep ocean.

Then Jas called out, 'Finn! That was awesome. You're amazing!'

And Amir said, 'You couldn't teach me to do that, could you, Finn – that leaping thing?'

Then came Charlie's voice, squeaky with anxiety. 'Pull in the sail, Amir. The wind's getting up. It'll drive us out to sea. It's going to be hard to get back to shore.'

Finn ducked his head under the water to listen longingly once more to the dolphins' departing whistle. Then he surfaced again and called out, 'Don't worry, Charlie. Give me the rope. I'll tow you.'

'I've seen it all now,' marvelled Charlie, throwing the bow rope overboard to Finn, who caught it expertly and tied it round his chest. 'You're right, Jas – we'll never be able to tell anyone about this. They'd think we were daft. I don't know what or who Finn thinks he is, but he can certainly swim like a dolphin, anyway. Let's get going, Finn. This wind's getting stronger.'

*

Neither Finn nor the three children in the *Peggy Sue*
saw the small knot of adults who had gathered on
the beach, anxiously watching the little dinghy come
storming back to shore.

Mrs Faridah was wringing her hands fretfully.

'You should not have given them permission,
Professor,' she
was saying.
'Children alone
out at sea like that.
It's too dangerous.'
'Mm, well,
Jas is usually
very reliable,'
Professor
Jamieson said
unhappily. 'I
do think it's
best to trust
children if
you can.'
M r
Munro
had been

staring out to sea, biting his lip as he watched the little boat, glancing up all the time at the sky where purple clouds were building up on the horizon. But as the *Peggy Sue* came scudding through the water, nearer and nearer to the beach, his face lightened and cracked into a broad grin.

'Look at that! Keeping a steady course with that wind behind him? Neatest bit of sailing I ever saw. You've no need to worry, Mrs Faridah, and you did the right thing to let them go out, Professor. My Charlie's a great little sailor, so he is. Nice one, son.'

Chapter Eight

Jas, Charlie and Amir were so busy fending off their parents that none of them had the chance to watch Finn. He managed to untie the rope as Charlie beached the dinghy, then he waded out of the sea after the others.

'Poor boy. Fell in, did you?' said Mrs Faridah. 'And you've lost your shoes, too. You need Amir to teach you how to go about in the water. He's a champion swimmer. Got a medal.'

Amir and Jas exchanged grins. Charlie turned and winked at Finn.

'Finn doesn't need swimming lessons,' he said. 'He's really amaz—Ow!'

A sharp kick in the shin from Amir warned Charlie to stop talking.

'I'll give you a hand getting the oars and stuff back to the harbour,' said Amir, changing the subject.

'OK. Finn'll help, won't you, Finn?' said Charlie, respect in his voice and friendship in his smile.

For a moment, Finn stared at him suspiciously. He'd been on the sharp end of Charlie's tongue and the business end of Charlie's fists all his life. But as he watched, Charlie's smile faded, to be replaced by a look of anxiety.

'Thanks for bringing the boat in,' he said in a quiet voice, keeping an eye on his father. 'You won't tell my dad it was you who did it, will you? And Finn, you are . . . you really are the most amazing swimmer I've ever seen in my life. World class. Olympic.'

He means it, thought Finn.

'Don't worry,' he said, trying to suppress a grin of triumph. 'I won't say a word.'

He grabbed a pile of life jackets out of the dinghy while Charlie started unscrewing the rowlocks.

'Watch out,' muttered Jas. 'Here comes trouble.'

Mrs Lamb was running down from the road above the beach towards them, waving her arms furiously.

'Where is she?' she was shouting. 'Where's my Kyla? What have you done to her?'

Jas started guiltily. It was obvious that she'd

completely forgotten about Kyla.

'She didn't want to come out with us, Mrs Lamb,' she said. 'She wanted to stay up there, in the lantern room.'

Everyone turned to follow her pointing finger. Kyla could be seen standing up in the little glass room at the top of the lighthouse, her hands pressed against the glass, looking down at them. Behind her mother's back, Jas beckoned urgently to her.

'What's she doing up there all on her own?' asked Mrs Lamb furiously. Have you children been mean to her?'

'No, honestly, Mrs Lamb,' said Amir soothingly. 'She was drawing a picture. She said she wanted to finish it.'

'Look. She's seen us. She's coming down,' said Jas.

Charlie had lost interest in Kyla. He'd started hauling the *Peggy Sue* further up the beach, out of reach of the waves, which were building up in the wind and crashing noisily on to the pebbles.

'I'll give you a hand,' said Finn.

It was strange to be talking to Charlie in a normal way. He half expected to be ignored, but Charlie said, 'Great, thanks, Finn.'

Together, they pulled the *Peggy Sue* a few metres up the beach. Jas and Amir ran up to them, leaving the adults clustered in a group, watching Kyla who was running over the dunes towards them.

'What's really going on?' Jas asked Finn quietly, when no one else was nearby. 'What happened to you in the sea? How come you can swim like that? How did you know about the dolphins and the balloons in the first place? All that stuff about the selkie – you were joking, weren't you? How did—'

'You've been having secret lessons, haven't you?' butted in Amir, who had come up behind them. 'I wish you'd tell me who your teacher is.'

Finn stopped their questions with a quick shake of his head.

'I wasn't joking. It's like I told you. My mother *was* a dolphin person. It's in the poem. Just read it again, and think about it. Look, I'll come round and tell you everything tomorrow if you like.'

'OK,' said Jas. 'In the lantern room, everyone. Straight after breakfast. Can you all do it?'

Charlie frowned. 'I have to help my dad on Saturdays on the *Janine*.'

'And I'm supposed to be clearing out my bedroom,' said Amir.

'Let's tell them we're doing a project,' said Jas. 'On – I don't know – on rock pools or something. We want to make a start.'

'On dolphins,' said Finn with a grin. 'Only I'm the only one who can research it.'

He saw the surprise on the others' faces, and then he laughed to himself inside as they smiled back at him.

'Here comes Kyla,' said Jas. 'I'll tell her. And I suppose we'd better let her bring Dougie. See you in the morning, everyone!'

Chapter Nine

When Finn woke up the next morning in his little bedroom under the eaves in the old cottage, he lay for a while wondering why he felt so happy. A fluttering by the window caught his eye. A butterfly had got trapped and was trying to get out. Finn jumped out of bed and opened the window to let it out.

The early sun shining on the sea almost dazzled him, and with the light came the memory of everything that had happened the day before. He'd saved the dolphins from the balloons! And he'd got the others to help him too. He grinned, remembering the respect and friendliness in Charlie's voice.

His heart sank a little as he remembered that he'd promised to go to the lantern room again today. Would the children still be friendly? He'd told them about his mum, but they hadn't seemed to believe him. He couldn't blame them. He could hardly believe it himself.

He turned back into his room and began to put on his clothes.

Meanwhile, over in the lighthouse and down in the cottages by the harbour, the other children were trying to persuade their parents to let them go to the lighthouse.

'What do you mean, you "can't" help me clean out the lobster pots?' Mr Munro was barking at Charlie as he fetched his jacket off the hook behind the cottage's front door. 'There's no *can't* about it. You're coming, and that's that.'

'It's for school, Dad,' said Charlie, trying not to let a tell-tale blush creep up his cheeks. He always went red when he told a lie. 'Like I told you – it's a project.'

'What project, darlin'?' said his mum.

'It's about rock pools,' said Charlie carefully, trying to remember the story the children had cooked up between them the night before. 'We're going to get . . .' He paused, fishing about in his memory for the right word.

'Specimens?' his mum said helpfully.

'That's it! Specimens!' Charlie nodded gratefully.

'No,' said Mr Munro.

'Yes,' said Mrs Munro. 'Education's important. Away you go, Charlie, but mind you're back in good time for your dinner. Twelve o'clock. No later.'

His older sister watched him with narrowed eyes as he jumped up from the table.

'You're up to something, I know you are,' she said.

'Am not,' said Charlie, and he dived out through the door as fast as he could to avoid further questioning.

'Well, I don't know, Kyla,' Mrs Lamb was saying, as she tied a satin ribbon round her daughter's ponytail. 'Look what happened yesterday, when they left you on your own for all that time. I don't think I trust those children. Are they being mean? Are you sure they're not bullying Dougie?'

'It's not like that at all,' said Kyla, pulling her head away from her mother's hands. 'We're going to be doing a project. For school. Amir'll be doing it too. And Jas. You like them. And I'll keep an eye on Dougie, I promise.'

'You don't want to go too, Dougie, do you?' Mrs Lamb had been spooning food into Buttons's bowl. She stopped and looked up, the spoon in mid-air. 'Not out there on the beach again on those nasty rocks? They're terribly slippery. Your knee's got a horrible graze from where you slipped on Thursday. Why don't I come with you? Just let me fix my make-up, and I'll—'

'You don't need to, Mum,' said Dougie, who had expected this and had prepared a way out. 'We're not going to be down at the beach much. We're going to be working at the lighthouse with Professor Jamieson. He's going to show us his . . . his . . .'

'Statistics?' said Kyla, throwing an admiring look at her little brother.

'Yes, *statsitstics*,' said Dougie, pouncing on the word, although he had no idea what it meant.

Meanwhile, Amir, of course, had to concoct a different story for Mrs Faridah, who would know perfectly well that she hadn't planned a school project on rock pools for her class.

'Really? You've decided to study rock pools?' she said suspiciously. 'All of you? Including Charlie Munro?'

'Yes, Mum,' said Amir, trying to look grown-up and important. 'Charlie was talking about the stuff his dad picks up in his lobster pots, and it started off the idea. It was Jas who suggested it.'

That bit's true, anyway, he told himself, looking at his mother with big, round, innocent eyes.

'Now that is very good,' said Mrs Faridah, looking pleased but mildly astonished. 'Jas is a very good student. You should get her father to help you. Professor Jamieson is a great expert, you know. He—'

'Yes, I know, Mum. In fact, that's where we're meeting. At the lighthouse.' Amir was poised at the door like an athlete on the starting line, his long legs itching to run up to the lighthouse. 'Can I go now? The others will be waiting for me.'

'All right,' said Mrs Faridah, 'but come back in time to clear up your bedroom, you hear? And don't get your shoes wet. Salt water is very bad for shoes. Maybe I'll come over to the professor's later to see how you're getting on.'

'No need, Mum!'

Amir was already running fast down the road.

*

'Dad,' Jas was saying, as she and her father munched their way through their toast. 'Can dolphins get hurt if they eat balloons?'

'That's a very good question,' replied Professor Jamieson enthusiastically. 'The rate of decomposition of the Mylar balloon is considerably longer than that of the latex. Both pose significant risks to marine life. The ingestion of balloons – and *thousands* are washed up on the beaches every year—'

'Yes,' interrupted Jas, 'but I just want to know what happens if a dolphin eats a balloon.'

Her father's eyes focused on her.

'I'm sorry, my dear. For a moment I thought I was talking to my students. Well, the balloon can block the dolphin's gut.'

'Will it die?'

'It may do.'

'But not always?' said Jas, thinking with horror of the dolphins who had already eaten the balloons before Finn had a chance to stop them.

'Not always. But if they eat a lot of junk – balloons, plastic bags, drinks bottles, plastic rubbish of any kind – their stomachs fill up with it. It's a very serious problem, Jas. The ocean's being clogged up with all sorts of plastic rubbish. Somehow or other, when people throw things away, a lot of it seems to end up in the sea. And it's not only dolphins who suffer, you know. Whales, porpoises, turtles, fulmars . . .'

'And then? What happens to them if their stomachs are full of plastic?'

'Well, my dear, I'm afraid to say that they starve. I've got a paper on it here somewhere. Let me see – under this pile . . . No, perhaps over there . . . Wasn't that a knock at the door? . . . Oh, hello, Charlie. You're early this morning. Amir, too! And there's a girl with a little boy running up behind you.'

A few minutes later, all five children were in the lantern room, breathlessly waiting for Finn, whose dad had cooked him a big breakfast, with bacon and eggs and toast.

'You know what, son?' said Mr McFee, pouring himself a cup of strong brown tea. 'It's an amazing relief knowing that I don't have to keep Sylvie's secret from you any longer. I've been that afraid. I feel like a new man today. We'll be all right now, won't we?'

'Yes, Dad, of course we will,' said Finn.

'Have the last piece of toast,' said Mr McFee, dropping it on to Finn's plate.

'I can't. I'm full,' groaned Finn. 'It was a great breakfast, Dad.' He pushed his chair back. 'I'll see you later.'

'Where are you going?' asked his father anxiously.

'To see my friends.'

'What friends? You haven't got any friends.'

'I'm not going back to sea today, Dad. It's OK,' said Finn. 'I'm meeting up with the others from my class at the lighthouse.'

'Where the barmy professor lives? You be careful, son. A scientist gets hold of you, and there'll be experiments and examinations and nosy parkers and journalists from all over. Let's keep all this to ourselves, eh? Our secret.'

'Sure we will, Dad,' said Finn, thinking guiltily about how he'd already told the other children. 'I'll be back before the football starts on the telly. I promise.'

'Here he is at last!' said Charlie as Finn's head popped up through the floor of the lantern room.

'We've told Kyla and Dougie. We had to,' said Jas. 'I hope you don't mind.'

'It's OK, but don't tell anyone else, please,' said Finn, whose father's warnings about scientists and nosy journalists had shaken him.

'We couldn't if we tried,' said Amir. 'Not if we don't want everyone to think we're crazy. I mean, all that selkie stuff. You had to be kidding us, weren't you, Finn?'

Finn felt his stomach drop.

It's hopeless, he thought. *They don't believe me. They'll just think I'm weirder than ever.*

Jas broke the silence.

'Sit down, Finn.

Look, there's a cushion for you. We want to know everything. I mean, how did you learn to swim like that? And all the leaping you did with that dolphin? You seemed to understand each other.'

'I didn't learn,' said Finn awkwardly. 'I found I could just do it. And I don't understand it any more than you do. I felt a kind of . . . well . . . a *change*, as soon as I fell into the sea. When I got home, I made my dad talk to me. He'd never told me about my mother. She died when I was only two. I don't remember her at all. But I knew, as soon as he told me she was a dolphin selkie, a dolphin woman, that it made total sense. I understood everything then: why I could swim; why I felt sort of different from the rest of you.'

'I just can't get my head round it,' said Amir. 'It's not . . . It's not *scientific*.'

'No, it's not. I know,' said Finn unhappily, not knowing what to say next. He looked round at the children's puzzled faces, and his eyes settled on Charlie, who was sitting a little apart from the others, leaning against the glass wall of the lantern room. The sun was right behind him, and Finn couldn't easily read the expression on his face. He knew what it would show though. Scorn and rejection.

But to his amazement, Charlie nodded.

'Not everything's scientific,' he said. 'I know what you mean, Amir. I thought that yesterday. But we were round at my grandda's last night. He was a fisherman all his life, so I asked him about selkies, and he knew all about them. He made sure my dad wasn't listening, then he said, "Believe me, Charlie, there's more in those old stories than you'd think. Lots of fishermen used to believe in selkies. Some still do, maybe. And who's to say they're not right, eh?" He's great, my grandda is. If he says something's true, I'll believe it.'

Finn felt almost weak with gratitude. He'd expected Charlie to be the hardest one of all.

'It sounds like a fairy story,' said Kyla happily. 'I love fairy stories. Especially when they have a happy ending.'

'My mum knows loads of stories like the selkie one from Pakistan,' said Amir. 'Magic ones, with jinns and that. My granny believes in them too. But I don't know. I mean, magic! It's not . . . not . . .'

'Scientific,' repeated Finn, finishing the sentence for him. 'I know. I'm having trouble believing in it too.'

'What happened to your mum, Finn?' said Jas gently.

She knows what it's like, thought Finn gratefully. *Her mum died too.*

Aloud he said, 'She was at sea. As a dolphin. She got caught in a fisherman's net. She died.'

'My dad told me about that,' said Charlie. 'He's accidentally killed dolphins a couple of times.' His eyes rounded with horror. 'Hey, I hope he didn't . . . I hope one of them wasn't . . .'

'It wasn't your dad,' said Finn. 'I know it wasn't.'

'How do you know she got caught in a net?' asked Kyla. 'I mean, you wouldn't know if it was her or just an ordinary one, would you? Your mum might still be out there in the sea.'

'My dad told me it was her,' said Finn shortly. 'He knew. He found her.'

He didn't say any more.

'My dad thinks your dad did away with your mum,' Dougie chipped in with relish.

'Shut up, Dougie!' the others chorused, turning shocked faces towards him.

Kyla, who was greedy for more sensational revelations, turned to Jas.

'Was your mum really an African princess?' she asked.

'Sort of. She was Ethiopian. There was royalty out there once. My mum was a cousin or something,' said Jas, looking solemn. 'My dad says so, anyway. He always called her his princess.'

Charlie pursed his lips, weighing up the evidence.

'That doesn't mean anything. My dad calls my mum a clucky old hen.'

'Got feathers on her bum then, has she?' sniggered Dougie.

There was a short silence. Jas broke it.

'Do you want to be in the Lighthouse Crew, Dougie?'

Dougie nodded anxiously.

'Then get this. We don't ever, ever, say anything bad about people's mums. *Ever.*'

'Sorry,' mumbled Dougie.

Thank you, Jas, thought Finn.

'What I want to know,' said Amir, 'is how you did that leaping.'

Finn squirmed uncomfortably.

'I can't explain it. When I'm in the sea, I'm different. I can see and hear things, and there's this sort of . . . power.'

'You are lucky,' said Kyla. 'I'm scared of the sea. I mean, when you think of all the things that could go wrong—'

'As well as the leaping,' Amir interrupted, ignoring Kyla, 'you seemed to understand what the dolphins were doing. Thinking, almost. Can you speak dolphin language?'

'I don't think they have a language. Not really,' said Finn. 'Not like us. They whistle and make clicking sounds. There was one – the one I met first – I can recognize his whistle. It's somehow different from the others.'

'I saw a programme about that. About animal communication,' said Amir enthusiastically. 'Did you know that parrots—'

'Do you mean the dolphin's whistle is like a sort of signature tune?' interrupted Jas.

'Yes! That's it exactly.'

Dougie had been sitting in red-faced silence. Now he blurted out, 'I'm really sorry I didn't invite you to my party, Finn. And I'm really sorry about the balloons, too. Mum didn't know it was a bad thing to do.'

'Nor did any of us,' Jas said kindly. 'It wasn't your fault, Dougie.'

'She got the idea off the local paper,' said Dougie. 'That new supermarket that's opening on Monday in Rothiemuir . . .'

'The one that's trying to put the village shop out of business,' said Kyla bitterly, 'and our mum out of work.'

'Yes, well, the grand opening's on Monday. On the Bank Holiday. And they're going to do a mass balloon release to advertise it. Five thousand red balloons! It's going to look amazing.'

A jolt of pure horror shot through Finn.

'Amazing? What do you mean, Dougie? It's horrible! *Awful!*' He was trembling with anger. 'Think how many dolphins five thousand balloons could kill!'

'And turtles,' said Jas. 'And whales, like my dad said.'

'And sea birds,' said Charlie. 'Dad finds dead ones sometimes. Because of the plastic bags and stuff.'

The children sat and stared at each other.

'We've got to stop them!' said Jas. 'But how?'

Chapter Ten

There was a long silence as everyone tried to think what to do.

'If we could get hold of some explosives,' Charlie said at last, 'we could blow up the supermarket building, then they wouldn't be able to have the opening ceremony at all.'

'Yes, and spend the rest of our lives in jail,' said Jas witheringly.

'How could we get any explosives?' said Amir. 'And anyway, wouldn't that be terrorism?'

'Miners use them down mines,' said Charlie doubtfully.

No one thought this was worth answering.

'Couldn't we just go and talk to them and *tell* them what would happen?' burst out Finn. 'Nobody wants to kill things, surely?'

'They wouldn't listen,' said Kyla bitterly. 'They don't listen to anyone. Mum's written loads of letters about how all the little shops will go out of business, but they don't care.'

'Yes, but killing *dolphins* . . .' said Finn.

'Anyway, they wouldn't believe us telling them how bad balloons in the sea are,' said Jas. 'Can you imagine them even bothering to talk to a bunch of kids?'

'I think we should get lots of dog poo and throw it at them,' said Dougie, who had stopped being awestruck by being in the Lighthouse Crew, and was his old self again.

'*Dou-gieee*,' chorused the others.

'This isn't a game, Dougie,' said Finn hotly.

'I'm only saying,' said Dougie, aggrieved.

'We'll have to start a campaign,' said Jas.

'There isn't time!' said Finn. 'Dougie said the ceremony's on Monday, and it's Saturday now! That's the day after tomorrow!'

The children sat in silence, thinking furiously. They were concentrating so hard, they didn't hear the footsteps coming up the ladder, and started with surprise when the trapdoor went up and

Professor Jamieson's head appeared.

'Which of you is Dougie?' he said.

'That's me,' said Dougie, looking anxious.

'Your mother's called to make sure you got here safely,' said the professor. 'She said you'd come to get some statistics from me?'

There was an embarrassed silence.

'I don't – exactly – know what *stateristics* is,' Dougie said at last.

'It's facts,' said Amir. 'Information.'

'We're doing a project,' said Charlie.

'On dolphins,' said Finn.

'No,' said Charlie. 'It's on rock pools.'

'You don't seem very sure,' said Professor Jamieson.

'The thing is, Dad,' said Jas, 'it's not exactly a project. More a . . . a protest meeting.' She saw the surprised look on the faces of the others, and said, 'Think about it. We haven't got time to do a project *and* sort out the balloon thing as well. We'd better just tell him. He might be useful.'

'Thank you, Jas,' her father said mildly. 'I'm always happy to help.'

'It's that awful new supermarket in Rothiemuir!' Kyla burst out. 'The one that's opening on Monday and that's going to put us out of business. They're going to release five thousand balloons!'

'It's wicked!' said Finn hoarsely. 'It's murder!'

Professor Jamieson looked grave.

'It is indeed appalling,' he said. 'I quite see that you need a protest meeting.'

'We're going to stop them,' said Dougie proudly.

'I see. May I ask how?'

'We don't know,' said Jas. 'We're still thinking.'

'Well, do you know, the simplest way is often the best,' said Professor Jamieson. 'Why don't I just phone them up and ask them to reconsider? We can go downstairs and I'll do it now, if you like.'

'They won't listen,' said Kyla. 'They never do.'

'Not to us,' said Jas, 'but there's a chance they might listen to my dad.'

Jas was used to her father's study, but the others looked round in awe. The big room was crammed with books and documents. The walls were covered with charts, maps and pictures, and a couple of impressive computers stood on the professor's desk.

Finn could hardly stand still, but the others were looking round curiously. Charlie was nodding knowledgeably at a map of the bay showing the

movement of currents. Kyla was admiring a picture
of a seal pup on the cover of a book. Amir's fingers
were clearly itching to have a go on one of the big
computers. Only Dougie had been distracted – by a
scab he was picking on his knee.

'Um – you don't happen to have a phone number
for the super-
market,
do you?'
said the
professor,
rootling
among the
papers on
his desk as
if he might
magically
find it
there.

Amir
pulled out
his phone
and scrolled
down it for a
few moments.

'Found it,' he said, holding it out to show him.

'Excellent piece of research,' said the professor. 'Have you considered a career in marine biology? I could—'

'Dad!' said Jas.

'Sorry,' said the professor. 'Now give me that number. Let's see what we can do.'

Finn held his breath as the professor, who had finally been put through to the manager of the new supermarket, politely explained that releasing 5,000 balloons would cause death and destruction to a large number of birds and animals. But it was clear that the conversation was not going well. As the voice on the other end of the line got louder and angrier, Finn balled his fists so tightly that his nails started digging into the palms of his hands. In the end, the professor was obliged to hold the phone away from his ear to avoid being deafened.

He replaced the receiver on the cradle and turned to face the children. Jas was shocked. She had never seen her father look so angry.

'Disgraceful!' said the professor. 'Stupid and irresponsible! And all because of some football player who's supposed to be at the opening.'

'A footballer?' said Charlie eagerly. 'Who?'

'Never heard of him,' said the professor crossly. 'Tom someone. Heston. Hetherton.'

'Not Tom Henderson?' breathed Charlie, exchanging looks with Amir.

'Henderson. Yes. The press will be there — newspapers, radio . . . This Henderson's supposed to be pressing the button to release the balloons. Of all the stupid — and it's the first time I've been called a crackpot, too. I shall make a strong complaint to the local council. Surely they must be able to put a stop to—'

'It's the weekend, Dad. It's Saturday. The offices will be closed,' Jas said unhappily. 'There's no time before the ceremony on Monday.'

'Then I shall send a strongly worded complaint to the environmental department,' said the professor. 'We must make sure it doesn't happen again. Now I'm sorry, children. I don't see what else I can do, and I have some urgent emails to attend to.'

'But we can't just . . . You c-can't just . . .' stammered Finn.

Jas made a face at him. Her father's attention had moved away. He was already thinking about something else.

The children filed silently out of the study and

climbed back up to the lantern room.

'Tom Henderson!' Charlie said reverently. 'In Rothiemuir! I don't believe it!'

'He's just the greatest,' said Amir. 'Did you see that goal in the last minute of overtime against Celtic? It sealed the match!'

'Shut up!' burst out Finn. 'What are you talking about football for? Don't you get how awful this is? I've got friends out there in the sea. They're probably going to die!'

'Sorry, Finn,' mumbled Charlie and Amir.

'I'm going to make a poster with a picture of a dolphin on it,' said Kyla, 'and put it up in our shop window.'

'That's a good idea, Kyla,' said Jas. 'Actually, it's a *great* idea. We can make loads of posters and stick them up all over Stromhead and Rothiemuir.'

'Yes, with a picture of a dolphin, and "Don't release balloons" written underneath.'

'No, it should say "Balloons kill dolphins",' said Finn passionately.

'It's not just dolphins, is it?' said Jas. 'It's birds. And seals. And everything.'

'How about "Balloons kill wildlife. Stop the balloon release!"' said Amir.

The others nodded.

'We'll need lots of sheets of paper and felt tips,' said Jas.

Charlie was looking uncomfortable.

'I dunno,' he said. 'I'm rubbish at drawing and writing.'

'We only need one really good one,' said Jas. 'Kyla's best at drawing. She can do it, and I'll make copies. Dad's got a really good printer. Then we can get the bus into Rothiemuir and put them up everywhere.'

'Mum'll never let us go to Rothiemuir without her,' said Dougie.

'You can leave that bit to Amir and Finn and me, then,' said Charlie grandly.

'What's the time?' Dougie said suddenly. 'Mum said I've got to be home by twelve. What are we going to tell her about the rock-pool project, and the . . . the data and everything?'

'We'd better drop that story,' said Amir. 'Just tell her we've changed our minds and we're setting up a – a . . .'

'A protest group,' said Jas.

Kyla nodded.

'She won't mind that. She'll be pleased. It's about

trying to save the village shop too.'

'But tell her we're going to save the dolphins as well,' said Finn, 'because somehow or other, we've just *got* to do it!'

Chapter Eleven

Finn ran all the way home, filled with rage and anxiety at the thought of the disaster that was only two days away. He was out of breath long before he got to the cottage on the cliff top.

I wish I was as strong on land as I am in the sea, he thought. *If I can't stop the balloon release, I'll have to go out to sea and find as many balloons as I can and gather them in by myself. But five thousand of them — they'll be blown for miles and miles! I'd never find them all.*

As he neared the cottage, he thought about his father.

I bet he hasn't really changed, he told himself. *He'll be doing nothing, as usual, just staring at the wall. He won't help me this time, either. He's never been any use.*

But when the cottage came into view, he stopped

short. That morning when he'd left home, the brambles and weeds in the garden had been the same as usual, growing up in a tangled jungle. Now they were lying in wilting heaps, and the windows, uncovered and washed, were glinting in the sunlight.

He really has changed! thought Finn jubilantly, bursting in through the door.

His father turned and smiled at him ruefully, holding up his left hand, from which blood was dripping on to the floor. 'Those stupid shears slipped, didn't they, while I was hacking away at all they weeds,' he said ruefully. 'I'd let my tools go all blunt and rusty. Going to have to sort myself out, eh, Finn?'

'Dad! It looks awful! Will you have to go to hospital?'

'Hospital!' scoffed Mr McFee. 'No need for that. Worse things happen at sea every day. There's an old first-aid kit somewhere, if I've had the sense to keep it. Top shelf in the kitchen. I'll sort myself out, no problem.'

It took Finn a while to clean his dad's hand, disinfect it and find a dressing, and while he ran about, looking for the first-aid kit and mopping his father's blood off the floor, Finn explained in breathless snatches about the balloon release.

To his dismay, the old defeated look came into his father's eyes.

'Oh son, that's terrible, that is,' he said. 'Those poor, innocent creatures, out there in the sea, helpless, and all for big supermarket bosses scrambling after money and . . .'

His eyes were watering, and now they strayed towards his greasy old chair, as if he was ready to sink back into it and shut out the world again.

'We're going to stop them, Dad. Me and the others,' said Finn hastily, trying to pull him back.

Mr McFee shook his head.

'There's no standing in the way of business, Finn. There's no fighting the big boys. Little people like us—'

'We're *going* to fight them!' Finn said passionately. 'I am, and my – my friends. We're making posters, and we're going to stick them up all over Rothiemuir and Stromhead.'

'Good for you, son,' said Mr McFee vaguely. 'Do you know what – all that gardening, it's worn me out. I'll just have a little sit down now, see what's on TV.'

'I'll get you a cup of tea then,' said Finn

automatically, and he went into the kitchen, put the kettle on and set about making his father a sandwich.

We'll just have to do it ourselves, he thought as he spread margarine on slices of bread. *Me and the Lighthouse Crew.*

Finn wasn't the only one who had been held up by events at home. Charlie, Amir, Kyla and Dougie were all pounced on by their parents as soon as they got through their front doors. Charlie had to clean out his dad's van, Amir had to tidy his bedroom, and Dougie had to help his mum water the roses while Kyla made a card for their gran's birthday. Even Jas was detained by Professor Jamieson. He had been mulling things over, and he now embarked on a rather (for him) detailed interrogation on why exactly she had gone out for a sail with Charlie when a squall was on its way, which led to a long lesson on the art and science of weather-forecasting.

'I've allowed you a great deal of freedom, my dear,' he said at last, his forehead wrinkling with anxiety. 'Stromhead is a safe place, with a good community, but I must be sure that I can trust you to make sensible decisions.'

It wasn't until three o'clock in the afternoon that

all of them had managed to escape. Jas had got out first. She'd gone round to the Lambs' cottage to see how Kyla was getting on with the poster. Kyla heard her feet crunch on the pebble path that led up the cottage's front door and came running out to meet her, waving a drawing in her hand. She handed it to Jas.

Jas stared in amazement at Kyla's picture of a leaping dolphin, with bright drops of water showering off it.

'Kyla, it's brilliant! It's beautiful!' she said.

'I did the drops with a silver pen,' Kyla said shyly. 'Do you really like it, Jas?'

Mrs Lamb appeared behind Kyla and put protective hands on her daughter's shoulders.

'You know, dear,' she said to Jas. 'I don't think you children have ever appreciated Kyla as much as you should. She's a very special—'

Kyla shook her off and rolled her eyes at Jas, who hid a sympathetic smile.

'Of course she's special,' said Jas, handing the poster back to Kyla. 'We do appreciate her, honestly. She's – well – she's one of the gang.'

'You see, Mum?' said Kyla. 'I keep telling you. They're my *friends*.'

Dougie squirmed past his mother, who was blocking the front door.

'I'm friends too, aren't I, Jas? I'm in the Lighthouse Crew. You said so.'

'Course you are, Dougie,' said Jas kindly. 'Can Kyla and Dougie come out now, Mrs Lamb? We're going to meet the others and get my dad to photocopy this poster. We want to put it up everywhere we can.'

'I suppose so,' said Mrs Lamb. 'Kyla's told me all about your campaign. Good luck is all I can say. I don't think it'll do any good, mind you. Those big business sharks don't listen to anyone. And I'm coming with you this time. You children have been running about without adult supervision for quite long enough today.'

Charlie and Amir were already down at the harbour when Jas and Kyla arrived, with Dougie trotting after them as fast as he could, towing Mrs Lamb.

'You see, Mum?' he said crossly. 'I *told* you the others were waiting for us. We've got important stuff to do.'

'It's a *campaign*,' panted a voice behind them. Finn was out of breath after sprinting all the way from

the cliff-top cottage. He held out his hand to Kyla.
'Have you done it? Can I see?'

He studied the poster for a moment, his head on
one side.

'It's good, Kyla. No, I mean it's amazing! I just
hope – I mean, it's *got to* work.'

'We're going up
to the lighthouse
to use my dad's
photocopier,' Jas
said. 'And . . . and
make some plans.'

Mrs Lamb
nodded
reluctantly.

'I'll come
and fetch
both you
little
lambs
at five
o'clock,'
she said
to Kyla.
'And,

Kyla, mind you look after Dougie.'

'Race you to the lighthouse!' shouted Amir, and all six children took off up the hill.

'See you later, Mrs Lamb,' Jas called out over her shoulder, then turned back just in time to grab Dougie's shoulder to stop him tripping over his shoe laces.

By four o'clock a neat pile of brightly coloured photocopies was on Professor Jamieson's desk.

'This is a very nice piece of work, Kyla,' Professor Jamieson said, picking up a copy and looking at it. 'Have you thought of a career in marine art? I'm sure . . . Oh! Is that the time? Excuse me, all of you. I've got an urgent phone call to make.'

Silently the children followed Jas up to the lantern room.

'We're running out of time!' burst out Finn as soon as they were all there. 'It's too late to get to Rothiemuir today.'

'That's right,' said Charlie. 'The last bus to get back to Stromhead leaves at six o'clock. We'd only just get there, and we'd have to come straight back.'

'I could ask my mum to take us in tomorrow,' said Amir. 'No point asking her tonight. My dad phones home on Saturday nights. She never goes out.'

'My dad won't be up to driving this evening either,' said Charlie. 'There's a social on at the Fisherman's Arms.'

'I'll get my father to take us in his van,' said Finn, hoping desperately that it was a promise he could fulfil. 'First thing in the morning.'

Charlie and Amir looked at each other, and Finn's lips tightened as he read their minds. He could tell that they were thinking of Mr McFee's old wreck of a van, which was always breaking down, and of Mr McFee himself – the suspected murderer.

'My dad wouldn't let me go off with your dad,' Charlie said with brutal honesty.

Finn flushed.

'Right. No problem,' he said bitterly. 'Suit yourselves. Me and him'll do the whole job on our own. Give me those posters, Kyla. We care more about dolphins than the rest of you put together anyway.'

He grabbed a stack of posters and disappeared through the trapdoor.

There was an uncomfortable silence after he'd gone.

'I'll see if my dad will give me a lift in too,' said Jas.

'If you go, Jas, Mum might let me come,' said Kyla.

'There's no way, no way at all, she'd let me . . .' began Dougie, then a smile spread across his face. 'But I could tell her your dad's taking us to the museum in Rothiemuir. She'd like that.'

'It wouldn't be a lie, anyway,' said Jas. 'They've got a noticeboard there. I'm sure they'd let us put up a poster.'

When Finn got home, he found his dad absorbed in the football on TV.

'Will you look at that, now?' he said admiringly as Finn came in through the door. 'That Tom Henderson, he's a wee marvel. Come here, son, and see the replay of this goal.'

Finn waited impatiently until the match was over, and then he showed him Kyla's poster.

Mr McFee held it out at arm's length and gazed at it admiringly.

'Beautiful!' he said. 'She must be a clever lassie. Where shall we put it, Finn? You can clear a space on the mantelpiece.'

'No, Dad. The Professor photocopied it. I've got a stack of them. I told you. I'm going to stick them up all over Rothiemuir and Stromhead first thing tomorrow morning. Can you take me in, Dad? In the van?'

Mr McFee scratched his head.

'Rothiemuir, eh? Haven't been there for years. I've avoided the place, if you must know. I wouldn't want to run into anyone I used to know in Rothiemuir.'

'Please, Dad,' begged Finn.

'Aye, well, I suppose,' he replied reluctantly. 'But don't get your hopes up, Finn. Your poster, it's very nice, but it won't make any difference.'

Finn hardly slept that night. His mind was full of horrible visions of dolphins tangled in balloon strings, slowly starving to death with their stomachs full of rubbish. He was out of bed at seven o'clock, and went to wake his father.

Mr McFee was dead asleep, and Finn had to shake him hard before he could get him to wake up.

'Please, Dad! You promised to take me into Rothiemuir!' he almost shouted. 'We need to get going! Now!'

Mr McFee sat up and stared blearily at his son.

'I couldn't get off to sleep till the wee small hours,' he groaned. 'I was that upset. I was thinking of all those poor creatures eating those balloons—'

'Coffee,' said Finn sternly. 'I'll get you some coffee. You have to get up, Dad. Now!'

It was an hour before Mr McFee's battered old van began to rumble down the lane towards Stromhead to pick up the road to Rothiemuir. Finn grabbed his father's arm as they reached the crossroads.

'Stop, Dad! There's Charlie and Amir!'

The van lurched to a halt.

'I'm coming with you,' said Charlie, looking defiantly over his shoulder towards the row of cottages where he lived.

'Me too,' said Amir.

Finn hopped out of the van and ran round to open the back doors.

'There's seats in there, sort of,' he said. 'You'd better strap yourselves in.

It was only ten miles to Rothiemuir, but when the van had finally come to a halt in the central car park, and Finn opened the back doors, Charlie and Amir stared at him speechlessly, their faces white.

'Does he always drive like that?' whispered Amir.

'Like what?' said Finn.

'Oh never mind,' said Charlie. 'Hey, isn't that the prof's car? Look — it is! And there are Kyla and Dougie. We're all here!'

Chapter Twelve

It was still quite early, and being a Sunday morning, Rothiemuir hadn't yet woken up. The six children stood in the car park staring round at the streets that radiated from the little town's central square, while Professor Jamieson and Mr McFee stood talking by the van.

'Well,' said Charlie, 'I suppose we should fan out and . . .' His voice trailed off uncertainly.

Finn had seen something.

'Look!' he said furiously, pointing to a big, brightly coloured poster in a shop window. It showed Tom Henderson in his football strip leaping up to kick a ball – only, instead of the ball, there was a balloon, and hundreds more were floating round his head.

Grand Opening of our Fabulous New Superstore! the

huge black letters spelled out. *Mass balloon release by Tom Henderson, Monday 3 p.m.!*

Finn was already halfway to the shop.

'We'll start right here,' he called back to the others. 'We'll stick our poster over . . .'

A horrible thought struck him, and he stopped so abruptly in his tracks that Jas, who had been following close behind, nearly ran into him. She smiled knowingly.

'You forgot to bring any sticky tape, didn't you? Don't worry. I've got lots of it. And scissors too.'

She couldn't help looking smug.

A few minutes later, Kyla's poster was taped to the outside of the window, covering up the middle of the supermarket's much bigger one, which was stuck on the inside. The children stepped back to admire it.

'I don't know,' began Kyla. 'It looks – well – not very *good* somehow.'

'Stop talking rubbish – it's brilliant!' said Jas encouragingly.

The others were running on down Rothiemuir's empty high street, looking from side to side to see where they could stick their posters on the grey granite walls and dusty shop windows.

'There's another one!' shouted Amir, pointing along the street to the post office.

The others hared after him.

They were sticking a poster to the window of a cafe when the owner came boiling out of it.

'Oi!' he was shouting. 'What do you kids think you're doing? This is vandalism, this is. Get out of here!'

Professor Jamieson and Mr McFee had had difficulty keeping up with the children. They came puffing along just as the cafe owner reached for Kyla's poster to tear it down.

'May I explain?' the professor said politely.

'No!' exploded the cafe owner. 'Are you in charge of these wee hooligans? You can clear out too.'

Professor Jamieson lifted his head and sniffed.

'Coffee,' he said. 'And fresh bread.' He took Mr McFee's arm. 'Perhaps my friend and I could come in and have some breakfast? I think, when you've heard our story, you might just change your mind.'

The cafe owner hesitated, but the prospect of two customers on a slack Sunday morning was too good to pass up. He stepped aside and let them in.

Finn was already heading off along the high street. Professor Jamieson stepped back outside and called after the running children, 'Stick together! Don't be too long, and be careful!'

The high street of Rothiemuir was slowly coming to life. Quite a few people were waiting at the bus station. Jas was about to stick a poster on the window of the ticket office when the glare of an inspector standing nearby sent her scurrying away.

A trickle of people were coming out of the church on the corner, and the minister, his white robes billowing around him in the morning breeze, was shaking them all by the hand.

Kyla went up to him. She was used to church. Her mother took her and Dougie to Sunday School sometimes at the chapel on the far side of Rothiemuir.

'Please can I stick this poster up on your noticeboard?' she asked the minister.

'What, my dear? What's it about?' said the minister, dropping the hand of the old lady who was telling him about her bad back.

'It's about the balloon release by the supermarket tomorrow afternoon,' said Kyla shyly.

The minister frowned.

'No thank you. We don't allow advertising on our noticeboard.'

'It's not advertising,' said Finn, running up. 'It's

about saving the dolphins. The balloons are going to kill them. It's so awful. We've got to stop it!'

He was feeling too much to get the words out properly.

The minister took the poster and read it.

'Who made these posters?'

'I did,' said Kyla. 'At least, I drew the picture.'

'It's excellent!' said the minister, smiling at her. 'Can you spare a few more? I'll show them to the congregation at our other services today and see if anyone will stick them up in their windows. Good for you. A fine community effort. Now why don't you come along to our youth service? Lots of fun, stories, singing – all that kind of thing.'

'Sorry, no time!' said Finn, thrusting a few posters into the minister's hands.

The others had raced off and were already round the corner and halfway down the road that led to the train station. Finn was chasing them when he became aware of heavy feet running after him.

'You, boy! Stop!' a man was shouting.

Finn looked over his shoulder. A couple of men were on his heels, and they didn't look friendly. Finn put on a burst of speed, but he'd only just rounded the corner when a heavy hand grabbed his shoulder.

The man spun him round and pinned him roughly against the wall. Finn's heart pounded with fright. Both men had bullet-like shaven heads and were dressed in black bomber jackets. They looked tough.

'This is what we think of you and your muck,' one of them snarled, grabbing the posters that Finn was carrying. Slowly and deliberately he began to tear them up, dropping the pieces into the gutter.

'Stop it! *Stop!*' yelled Finn. 'You can't do that! We've got to save the dolphins, and the birds, and the – the seals!'

'Says who, yer wee

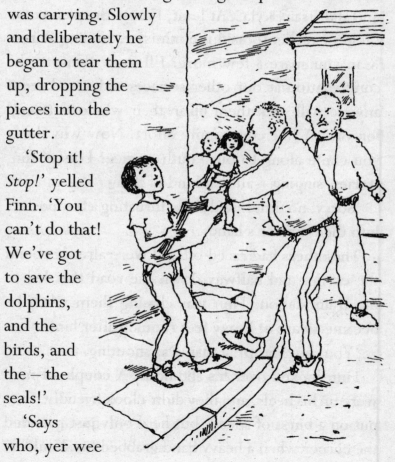

criminal?' said the first man. 'Someone put you up
to this. Animal rights, eh? Animal terrorists, more
like. Sabotage against a legitimate business, that's
what this is. There's laws against it. We'll get you
done. Youth custody, that's where you're heading.'

In the distance, Finn heard Charlie shout, 'Hey,
Finn's in trouble! Come on!' Then there was the
sound of racing footsteps as the five other children
came running up.

'That's handy,' one of the men said with a laugh.
'All of them together. Get the posters off them,
Nige.'

There was a brief scrum as the two men tore the
remaining posters out of the hands of the others.
Then, as the children watched helplessly, they ripped
them all to shreds. Soon, only a mound of torn paper
lay on the pavement.

'And don't think we've missed any around town,'
Nigel jeered. 'We've been following you. We've
taken down every one. You think you're going to
stop the new supermarket, you've got another think
coming. We've got jobs lined up there. Good pay,
too. We're in charge of security. Know what that
means? It means we've been trained to deal with
troublemakers. We know what to do with kiddie

criminals, don't we, Barry?'

'Aye, so we do,' said the other. 'Damned anarchists, that's what you are. Out of order. Come on, Nige.'

Laughing, they sauntered off.

Finn's face was red with rage. He wanted to run after them and pummel their retreating backs with his fists, but before he could move, Charlie and Amir had each grabbed one of his arms to stop him.

'Give it up, Finn,' said Amir. 'They're just too strong.'

'They're . . . they're disgusting,' said Kyla. Her eyes were brimming over with tears. 'My lovely posters!'

Dougie had retreated and was hiding in a doorway. Jas saw him peeping out.

'I want to go home, Jas,' he whispered.

'It's all right. They've gone,' said Jas. 'Come on. We'd better go back to the cafe and tell my dad and Mr McFee. I'm so sorry, Finn. We tried.'

'And we're not giving up!' Finn said savagely. 'We've got to think of something else, that's all.'

All the way along the high street, the posters they had so carefully put up had been ripped down and were lying trampled and torn on the pavement. But as they crossed the road, with the cafe straight in front of them, Kyla let out a cry.

'Look! In the window!'

The supermarket's poster had gone from inside the cafe window, and Kyla's was now in its place.

The children hurried inside. Professor Jamieson and Mr McFee were sitting at a table with empty cups and plates in front of them, and the cafe owner was leaning against the counter, smiling.

'Here they come!' he said, watching as they all trooped in. 'Eco-warriors! Good for you, kids. I've heard all about it from these gentlemen, and it's a right shame, so it is.'

'Dad!' burst out Jas. 'Two men were following us and they ripped all the posters down and nearly beat up Finn!'

'Ha,' said the cafe owner. 'I know those two. Couple of bullies. Always causing trouble round town. I heard they'd been hired by the new place. They tried to take your poster down from my window, but I sent them packing.'

'What's that?' said Mr McFee, starting up from his seat. 'Where are they? Bullying the kids? I'll . . .'

He subsided again as Professor Jamieson put a hand on his sleeve.

'Is everyone OK?' said the professor, throwing a searching look round the group of children. 'Did they hurt any of you?'

'No, honestly, Dad,' said Jas. 'We're fine.'

Her father got to his feet.

'It's time we got going, anyway,' he said, shaking the cafe owner's hand. 'Thank you. An excellent breakfast.'

'Come on, come on,' Finn was saying impatiently, leading the way to the car park. 'We've got to get back to Stromhead and make another plan. We *must*!'

The others ran after him – all except Jas, who had dropped the sticky tape and had stopped to pick it up. She overheard her father say, 'Well, Mr McFee, have you ever thought of working in property maintenance? Having been at sea, I guess you're a practical man. There are some rather urgent matters that need seeing to around the lighthouse.'

Jas put on a spurt and caught up with Finn.

'I think my dad's just offered your dad a job,' she said breathlessly.

Finn's jaw dropped, but then he shook his head.

'He can't have. Nobody ever would.'

The thought of his father going off to work was too weird to take in. He put it out of his mind, and his brows creased again as he racked his brains, trying to think of another way to stop the balloon release.

Chapter Thirteen

Back in Stromhead, the children tumbled out of Professor Jamieson's tidy little car and Mr McFee's ramshackle van and went to perch on the harbour wall. Finn couldn't bear to sit alongside the others. He stood in front of them, hopping from one foot to the other, too upset to keep still.

'It's no good,' Jas said bitterly. 'They've won.'

'They *can't* win! They *mustn't!*' burst out Finn.

'I told you what they were like, didn't I?' said Kyla.

Charlie was sitting awkwardly with his arms crossed over his chest.

'What's that poking up out of your T-shirt?' Amir asked him.

Charlie blushed.

'Nothing.'

'It's not nothing. It's paper. Rolled up. Go on. What is it?'

He leaned over and tried to prise Charlie's arms off his chest.

'Leave me alone!' panted Charlie. 'I told you. It's nothing.'

But Jas had recognized a corner of the paper that Charlie was trying to hide.

'It's the supermarket poster, isn't it?' she said accusingly. 'Of Tom Henderson and the balloons.'

Charlie gave up trying to hide it. Reluctantly he pulled it from under his T-shirt and let it unroll.

'So what, anyway?' he blustered. 'It's a great picture of him. I'm going to cut round the bit with him in it, and get rid of all the balloons, and stick it up in my bedroom.'

'Traitor,' muttered Amir, but he was looking enviously at the poster.

Everyone glanced nervously at Finn, expecting him to explode in anger, but he was staring at the poster of Tom Henderson, frowning with concentration.

'What's he like?' he asked Charlie.

'Who?'

'Tom Henderson.'

'He's the best!' Charlie looked relieved. 'That goal, against Rangers last season . . .'

'And the one in the Scottish FA cup semi-final two years ago was—' began Amir.

'Shut up about goals and stuff,' said Finn. 'What's he *like*?'

'He's . . . he's just *great*,' said Charlie.

Finn bounced impatiently on the balls of his feet.

'I think I can see what Finn's getting at,' said Jas. 'If he's a nice person, I mean, if he—'

'If he cares about anything at all, except for stupid football,' said Finn.

'Stupid? You think football's *stupid*?' said Charlie hotly.

Finn ignored him.

'Like I said – if he cares about anything important, he might refuse to do it. Release the balloons, I mean. If we could just get hold of him somehow! Persuade him!'

'We could never do that.' Amir was shaking his head. 'Top footballers like him, they have guards and minders and stuff.'

'How's he getting to Rothiemuir, anyway?' Finn said urgently.

'He'll have a smashing car, you bet,' said Charlie.

'A stretch limo with all white leather seats and a TV.'

'You think we might be able to stop his car when he's on the way here, is that it, Finn?' asked Jas.

Finn nodded unhappily.

'I was thinking that, but it's crazy, I know. I've got no idea how we'd do it, but it could be our only chance.'

'We don't even know what his car looks like,' objected Kyla.

Amir had been fiddling with his phone. He gave a triumphant 'Yes!' and held it out for the others to see.

'Ferrari!' he said. 'He's got three cars, but it says here that this one's his favourite. The picture even shows the number plate: TH1.'

'I don't see how it helps,' said Kyla. 'How are we going to stop him while he's driving along a main road? There'll be loads of other traffic, and he'll be going really fast in a car like that. It'd be much too dangerous to try and stop him.'

'Hey! I don't believe it!' said Amir, who was still staring at his phone.

'What?' Finn was dancing with impatience. 'Is it good? What does it say?'

'Wait till you hear this,' Amir said triumphantly.

'*Tell* us!' pleaded Finn.

'He won't be coming by the main road,' said Amir. 'This website's got all sorts of stuff about him. You won't believe this, but his granny lives in Tamsy Bay!'

'Tamsy Bay? That's where my Uncle Jimmy lives!' said Charlie. 'He's got a flat right down near the beach.'

Finn was thinking furiously.

'The road from Tamsy Bay to Rothiemuir's really small and winding and it runs right past my house. There's never any cars on it. I bet he'll be staying with his granny tonight.'

'You can't be sure though,' said Dougie, concerned. 'He mightn't like his granny. I don't like mine much. She's always trying to kiss me.'

Everyone ignored him.

'Of course he'll be staying with her,' said Finn, slapping his forehead. 'Think about it. Why would he come all this way to open a stupid supermarket in a little town like Rothiemuir? It can only be to please his granny. The ceremony's at ten o'clock tomorrow morning. To get here from anywhere else, by plane or something, he'd have to leave really early in the morning.'

'I wouldn't open that supermarket even for my granny,' said Kyla. 'I'd just throw a pot of paint at it if they asked me.'

'Yeah, but no one's going to ask you, silly,' said Charlie.

'Finn's right,' said Jas. 'It's the only thing that makes sense. The question is—'

'How do we get to him and persuade him not to release the balloons?' interrupted Finn.

'I bet his granny's got a cat,' said Dougie, flailing his padlock around on its chain as if he wanted to hit something. 'Mine's got three. We could kidnap her cat and say we won't give it back unless he promises not to release the balloons.'

Jas rolled her eyes.

'Firstly,' she said, ticking the points off her fingers, 'we don't even know where his granny lives, never mind if she actually has a cat. Secondly, even if she did have one, she'd be really, really upset if it got kidnapped. Thirdly, cruelty to animals—'

'I was just saying,' said Dougie, offended.

Finn was still thinking hard.

'You're right, Jas. We don't know where Tom Henderson's granny lives, and even if we did, it's eight miles to Tamsy Bay. We haven't got time to get there. Anyway, his minders would never let us near him. So that means . . .'

'It means we'll have to stop his car on the road somehow,' Jas finished for him.

'That's right,' said Finn. 'But how?'

Everyone thought.

'We could scatter nails on the road and he'd get punctures and have to stop to fix them,' said Charlie.

'That's criminal damage or something, isn't it?' said Amir. 'And anyway, punctures can take ages. He might be miles further down the road before he even notices.'

'I would lie down in the middle of the road if that's what it would take to stop him,' said Finn passionately.

'But he'd run over you,' said Kyla. 'Oh please don't, Finn. That's so dangerous!'

'I wouldn't care.'

'It wouldn't help the dolphins if you were dead,' Amir said reasonably.

'I could make another poster,' said Kyla, 'and hold it up.'

'He'll be in a Ferrari.' Charlie's voice was withering. 'He'd be past us in flash. A poster would just be a blur.'

'No, but it's a good idea,' said Finn eagerly. 'Only we'd need not just one poster, but lots, spread out, so that he'll have time to take them in. There's loads of bends on the road up to my house. He'll have to slow down.'

'We could paint something on the road,' said Amir, catching his enthusiasm. 'Something like "Tom Henderson – please stop and save the dolphins".'

'That won't make any sense to him,' said Jas. 'We've got to make him *want* to stop. Make him curious.'

'Like "Please stop because we've got something to tell you",' suggested Dougie.

'He'll think we're just fans wanting autographs,' said Charlie. 'Mind you, I wouldn't mind asking for one, if we do get to meet him.'

'We can have a *series* of messages, one on each bend,' said Finn. 'The first one goes, "Tom Henderson, we have something very important to tell you." The second one, on the next bend, says, "Please stop. This won't take a minute." The third one goes, "Lives are at stake." The fourth one says, "We're not just football fans wanting your autograph."'

'That's no good,' said Amir. 'He'll be insulted if

we say we don't want his autograph.'

'All right – leave that one out,' said Finn.

Kyla was looking worried.

'I haven't got time to draw all those posters,' she said.

'You won't have to,' said Jas. 'We don't need pictures, just words, in very big letters. Hey, Dougie, here comes your mum. She's looking a bit upset. It's past one already! We'd better go, but come to the lantern room, as soon as you can this afternoon!'

Kyla, Amir, Charlie and Dougie jumped off the harbour wall and ran off home, leaving only Jas and Finn, who was standing by himself, looking out to sea. Jas went up to him. Finn heard her coming, but didn't turn round.

'It's the best we can do, Finn,' said Jas. 'It might work.'

'I keep thinking about them out there,' Finn said hoarsely. 'All tangled up and eating rubbish, and getting sick, and starving. If those balloons go up, Jas, I'm going to go back out to sea and gather up as many of them as I can myself.'

'Five thousand balloons?' said Jas. 'You can't, Finn! They'll be all spread out over miles and miles!'

'I know, I know. I just feel so sad for them. And sort of responsible in a way. Those dolphins! I've only met them a couple of times, but they're my friends.'

'You've got other friends now, in case you hadn't noticed,' said Jas in a small voice.

He turned to look at her, and for a moment, neither of them spoke.

'Can you remember your mum, Jas?' Finn said eventually.

She looked at him, startled.

'You lost your mum too,' she said. 'I never — I didn't think . . .'

'Yes, but do you remember her?' She shook her head.

'Only a bit. Not much, anyway. She was – she was soft and warm, and she told me stories, only I can't remember any of them. I can still just about feel what it was like being cuddled up to her while she talked.'

'I don't remember anything at all,' said Finn. 'Only a feeling of being lost after she'd gone.'

His face looked set and stony. She touched his arm.

'Loads of people lose their mums, Finn. We've got our dads, haven't we?'

She stopped, and bit her lip as a picture of Finn's father came to mind, with his shaggy hair and dirty clothes and angry voice.

But to her surprise, Finn brightened.

'Yes, I've got my dad. And he's OK. At least, I think he is. I think he might be changing, Jas. You'll see.'

Chapter Fourteen

That evening, Finn went up to his bedroom soon after supper, but he couldn't sleep. It was almost June, and the sun would linger on the horizon until after nine o'clock. He watched the light slowly fade as he knelt at his bedroom window looking out over the sea.

'I wish I could come out now, just to be with you,' he whispered. 'I promise I'll come tomorrow, and if I can't stop the balloons, I'll do my best to lead you away from danger.'

He went back to bed and shut his eyes, but horrible images of sick and dying dolphins filled his mind.

Finn slept fitfully. He lay still for a moment, yawned, and was about to turn over and go back to sleep when a jolt ran through him. He had to get up and catch Tom Henderson! Had he left it too late?

There was a battered old clock on the shelf above his bed. He grabbed it and read the time. It was half past seven already!

He leaped out of bed, threw on his clothes and almost tumbled down the steep, narrow stairs into the kitchen below.

He'd planned everything with Jas the night before. She and Charlie had promised to be at the cottage early to help, but he didn't dare believe that they'd really come. He'd hoped, too, that his dad would be up, but the heavy snores coming from upstairs were discouraging. It would take too long to get his father up and going, and he hadn't got time to waste.

The placards the children had prepared yesterday afternoon were stacked by the kitchen door. He looked through them. He'd thought they were good last night. Now they looked childish and pathetic. But while he'd been asleep, his dad had nailed them to some old splintered battens to make them easier to display.

'Thanks, Dad,' Finn said softly.

He slung his bag over his shoulder, picked up the placards, and pushed open the cottage door. The low morning sun, reflecting off the sea, was so dazzling that he had to shut his eyes against the light.

'Finn!'

Had he imagined it, or was someone calling?

'Finn!' the voice came again.

He opened his eyes and saw Jas running up the road towards the cottage with Charlie a few paces behind. Relief pumped through him. They'd come after all.

Charlie was staring at the front of the cottage.

'What's happened? It looks different.'

'Dad's been cutting stuff back,' Finn said shortly. 'Here, take these. Mind out for splinters on the wood. We only had these old bits.'

He led the way out through the broken gate with Jas close behind him.

'I was looking for good places on the way here from Stromhead,' she said bossily. 'I suggest that we start . . .'

Finn shook his head.

'It's better the other way, towards Tamsy Bay. There are loads of bends and good places to put up the placards. I went to have a look last night. Hey, watch out!'

A car was coming fast along the narrow road. The children had to press themselves into the hedge at the side to avoid it.

'And that was only a Ford Fiesta,' said Charlie disgustedly. 'Think what Tom Henderson's Ferrari will do!'

'Come on!' called Finn over his shoulder. 'We haven't got much time!'

The first bend wasn't far off. Finn pointed to a wizened old tree, bent over by the sea wind, on the corner.

'That's the best place. You can see it clearly when you come round the bend. I tried looking.'

Jas was biting her lip.

'I'm sorry, Finn. I've only got sticky tape. It won't work on a tree trunk.'

Finn shook his bag. It rattled.

'No need for tape. Dad got out nails and a hammer.'

Charlie tried to grab a placard from him.

'I'd better do the nailing,' he said. 'I'm brilliant at it, and you'd only bash your thumbs. Give me the hammer, Finn.'

'Wait, Charlie!' said Finn. 'You've got the wrong placard! They've got to go in the right order!'

'Well hand the right one over then.'

Finn put the placards on the ground and sorted

them out. He picked up the last one, which said, *Please stop here, Tom! We really need to talk to you!* and handed it to Charlie.

Charlie was good at nailing, and a second or two later the placard was in place.

'Watch out! A car's coming!' Jas called out. 'Maybe it's him!'

But the car was only a battered old Vauxhall. It braked sharply at the bend, and the children could see the driver frowning at the placard. 'It's old man

Wilson from the farm,' said Finn. 'He hates me and my dad.'

He held his breath, half expecting Mr Wilson to get out of his car and rip the placard down. He only breathed out again when he saw the car chug on.

'Next one!' he shouted, and the others dashed after him.

Half an hour later, all the placards were in place, and a few more cars, a van and a tractor had passed. None of them had stopped, though they had all slowed down. It was obvious that the placards were catching the drivers' attention.

'We'd better get back to the bend nearest my house,' panted Finn, who had been on tenterhooks as Charlie methodically hammered the placards on to trees, fence posts and field gates. 'That's where we want him to stop.'

As he ran back past each placard, he checked them, hardly aware of the others on his heels.

I'd stop if I was Tom Henderson, he told himself. *I'd want to know what it was all about.* He recited the messages under his breath as he ran.

Tom Henderson!!! These messages are for you!
We have something very important to tell you!

We don't just want autographs.

When you release the balloons, you will be putting lives in danger.

Please stop here, Tom! We really need to talk to you!

It was here, where the last placard was nailed to the old tree, that he wanted Tom Henderson to stop. He came to a halt and put his hand on the tree, trying to catch his breath. The thoughts that he'd been pushing away broke through at last.

'We might have got it all wrong!' he wailed, as the other two caught up with him. 'What if he's not staying with his nan? What if he's coming in a helicopter? He might *easily* be! What if—'

'Shut it, Finn,' said Charlie. 'A car's coming. Listen.'

They stood, faces pale with anxiety, straining to listen. But instead of the smooth, expensive hum of a Ferrari, they could hear the raucous rumble of a diesel engine. And it kept stopping. Car doors were banging, and there were sounds of men shouting and wood splintering.

And then it appeared. A dirty white van. It shuddered to a stop beside the three children. The doors swung open, and out stepped the two men who had pulled Kyla's posters down the day before in Rothiemuir.

'Well, look who's here, Barry,' said one.

'Might have known it, eh, Nige?' said the other.

'It's a disgrace, wouldn't you say?' said Nigel.

'It is that,' said Barry.

'Lucky we came this way to work,' said Nigel.

'Dead right, or we might have missed this mess.'

'A mess, aye – it's a mess, this is. And what do we do with a mess?'

'We clean it up, Barry.'

Nigel strode to the tree and with a powerful tug ripped the placard off it. Then he swore loudly.

'Yer wee vandals! It's given me splinters! All over my hands! Look!'

'Serves you right!' Finn shouted hotly. Tears were streaming down his cheeks. 'You're murderers! You don't even know what you're doing!'

'Oh, we know.' Barry was advancing on him. 'We're sorting you out, that's what we're doing.'

Finn ran at him, the blood pounding hard in his ears. He was much smaller and slighter than Barry, but he was driven by such rage that he took the big man by surprise and nearly knocked him over.

But Barry recovered quickly. As he righted himself

and lurched forward, his elbow hit Finn in the ribs. Finn doubled over, winded, hardly able to breathe. He was dimly aware of Jas and Charlie standing up to the other man, who was jeering at them loudly.

Finn tried to stand upright, but Barry caught hold of his forearms and held them up in front of his face in a tight grip.

'Let go of me! Let *go*!' shouted Finn. 'You don't understand! The dolphins—'

'I'll give you dolphins, you little—' snarled Barry. He stopped abruptly at the screech of expensive tyres squealing to a halt behind him.

'Oi! You! What are you doing? Let that kid go!'

Finn's hands were suddenly released. He stood, dazed, rubbing his wrists, and stared at a tall, muscular young man who had stepped out of a green Ferrari and was looking down at him with concern in his eyes.

'Tom!' croaked Finn. 'You're Tom Henderson! Please, you've got to stop them. They're going to be killed!'

'What? Who's going to be killed? Stop who? Are these men hurting you?'

Nigel and Barry were looking at Tom in awe.

'We done nothing, Tom. It's them kids. They're

vandals. Putting up posters and that all over the place. We love kids, don't we, Nige?'

'Course we do, Barry. Any chance of giving us an autograph, Tom? That last goal, against Rangers, it was . . . it was . . .'

'Awesome,' said Barry reverently.

Tom was looking from one to the other through narrowed eyes.

'One thing I can't stand is bullying. I saw you having a go at this boy. You should be reported. Threatening behaviour, that's what it was.'

'Just one little autograph,' pleaded Nigel. 'Mean a lot to me, it would.'

'Get out of here,' Tom said angrily. 'I told you. I can't stand bullies.'

Barry was tugging at Nigel's sleeve.

'Leave it, Nige. Let's go. We'll be late for work as it is.'

Looking back awestruck at Tom Henderson, Barry dragged Nigel away, and a minute later he had crunched the van into gear and it had hurtled off.

'It's the dolphins,' said Finn hoarsely. 'The balloons – Oh please, Tom, I've got to tell you!'

Someone else had come up behind the footballer.

'Time's getting on, Tom,' the man said. 'Can't

keep everyone in Rothiemuir waiting.'

'Give us a minute, Sam.'

Tom Henderson put his hand down and helped Finn to his feet.

'You haven't got a minute,' grumbled the other man.

'Oh please,' begged Finn. 'I've just got to tell you. It's a matter of life and death.'

Tom Henderson looked at him, scratching his head.

'Tell you what,' he said at last. 'Hop into the car. You can tell me all about it on the way into Rothiemuir.'

Charlie, who had been standing by, too awestruck to move, found his voice.

'Can I come too, Tom, please?'

But the car doors had already shut, and it was speeding off down the lane.

Chapter Fifteen

The back seat of the Ferrari, although cramped, was the most luxurious thing that Finn had ever seen, but he didn't even notice the creamy white leather and the soft padded fittings. He was still shaken up by his encounter with Barry, but he was horribly aware of how fast the car was going as it purred swiftly towards Rothiemuir. He had only a few minutes to put his case to Tom Henderson.

Tom was sitting in the passenger seat. He turned to look back at Finn.

'So what's this all about then? Why were those goons getting at you? What's your name, anyway?'

'I'm Finn.' Finn's voice came out in a croak. He cleared his throat and tried again. 'We'd – me and my friends – we'd set up some placards for you to see because we desperately wanted to talk to you.'

'Matter of life and death, you said.'

'Yes! It's the balloons, see.' Finn was frantically trying to sort out his thoughts. Why hadn't he planned what he was going to say?

'What's he talking about?' Sam, Tom's driver, changed down a gear as he eased the car out from the coastal lane on to the main road into Rothiemuir. 'He's having you on, Tom. Kids'll do anything for an autograph. You shouldn't have picked him up.'

'No!' Finn almost shouted. 'It's the balloons, see, they'll blow out to sea and land on the water and when the air comes out of them, the dolphins will think they're jellyfish and eat them. Their stomachs get all filled up with balloon rubbish and they won't be able to eat anything. They'll starve!'

'Sounds daft to me,' said Sam. 'Balloons don't look a bit like jellyfish. And even if they do eat them, they'll just poo them out again. I swallowed a fridge magnet when I was kid. Came out the next day with a clunk into the toilet.'

'They can't poo them out! They don't!' Finn was watching with horror as the car sped through the outskirts of Rothiemuir, coming closer to the supermarket. 'Their insides aren't like ours. And the balloon strings get wrapped round their mouths and their fins.'

'That's quite interesting, that is,' said Tom. 'I didn't know about all that.'

'Careful, Tom,' Sam said. 'You don't know what you might get into.' His eyes met Finn's in the mirror. 'You an eco-warrior?'

'A what?' said Finn.

'Animal rights nutter.'

'I'm *not* a nutter!' burst out Finn hotly. 'I just – I care about dolphins. I've *seen* one all tangled up in a balloon string. It was horrible.' He stopped, racking his brains for anything else that could impress the footballer. 'And it's not just dolphins. It's seals, and turtles, and lots of other wildlife too.'

The huge square bulk of the supermarket was now visible ahead.

'We'll have to let you out here, Finn,' Tom said kindly.

'Yes, but will you do it?' begged Finn.

'Do what?' said Tom, looking puzzled.

'Say you can't let the balloons go, to save the dolphins!'

'Are you joking?' scoffed Sam. 'I can see it now, can't you? Tom Henderson rolls up, cameras popping, journalists got their mikes out, provost steps up, chain round his neck, and Tom says, "Oh sorry, guys, I can't let your balloons go up because of some kid I've never met before who told me not to.""

The car whispered to a halt. Sam got out and opened the door, waiting for Finn to follow. Dry sobs were rising in Finn's sore throat.

'Please, Tom,' he pleaded. 'Please.'

'Sorry, Finn. Can't do it,' said Tom. 'It's all been set up, ages ago. You know what? You worry too much. I bet it's not nearly as bad as you think. They wouldn't allow it if it was that awful, would they? Tell you what, I'll give you my autograph and a couple of extras. You can swap them with your mates. Get yourself a treat, eh?'

He reached for a pad in the car's glove pocket and began to scribble his name.

'Out,' said Sam, reaching into the car to grab Finn's arm. 'Now.'

'It's all right, Sam,' said Tom. 'He's a good kid. Means well, I can see. May have a point, too. Tell you what, Finn, I'll donate my fee for doing this to charity, OK? Save the Whales, or something.'

He held out some bits of paper to Finn with his

autograph on them. Finn shook his head mutely. He was too choked up to speak.

Seconds later, Sam had hauled him out of the car and he was standing on the pavement, while the Ferrari hummed away towards the crowd that was waiting outside the supermarket.

Finn had never felt so miserable in his life.

I'm useless, he thought. *Everything I do goes wrong. I'm just a stupid—*

'Finn!' he heard someone call. 'What happened? What did he say?'

He turned to see Jas and Charlie stepping out of his father's ancient van. They ran up to him.

'What's he like?' said Charlie breathlessly. 'And did he give you his autograph?'

'Yes he *did*,' said Finn savagely, 'and I shoved it back at him. He's useless and stupid, just like me.'

'He gave you his *autograph*? And you didn't take it?' said Charlie, shocked.

'He wouldn't listen to you, then,' said Jas sadly.

'You should have taken it and given it to me,' Charlie said bitterly. 'You should have let me go with him, anyway. I'd have talked to him about football. Got him on our side. Nudged him in the right direction.'

'Are you crazy? There wasn't time. That car, it goes so quickly and quietly, you don't even know it's moving. We were here in no time.'

'Not like your dad's van then,' said Charlie. 'We were shaken to bits.'

'But it was nice of him to give us a lift,' said Jas, frowning at Charlie. 'He drove past us on his way to Stromhead. Said he was going to meet my dad here to talk about his new job. I don't know what . . .'

She stopped, as neither of the boys was listening to her. Finn had subsided into defeated misery. Charlie was still brooding on the lost autograph.

'Come on, you two,' she said briskly. 'We can't stand here all day.'

'Come on where?' said Finn. 'There's no point in going anywhere.'

'To the supermarket, that's where,' said Jas.

'What on earth for?'

'You never know. Something might happen. We might get another chance. Tom Henderson might change his mind at the last minute.'

'He might be signing autographs, but I bet there'll be a queue a mile long,' said Charlie, shooting a sour look at Finn.

Jas and Charlie set off.

I'll go down to the beach, thought Finn, *and I'll see which way the wind's blowing. If the balloons start coming down on the water, I'll go out and start getting them in.*

Somehow, though, he couldn't bear the idea of being alone. Almost without knowing what he was doing, he turned back and began to follow Charlie and Jas.

There was a big crowd outside the supermarket. The people of Rothiemuir had come out in force, and half of Stromhead had turned up too. Finn could even see Mrs Lamb's blonde head at the back of the crowd, with Kyla and Dougie bobbing up and down beside her, alongside Mrs Faridah.

'I can't wait to get in there and start shopping,' Finn heard a woman say. 'There's a fresh bakery and offers on everything.'

The Ferrari had pulled up just past the supermarket door. A red carpet had been laid out, and the provost was standing on it, his gold chain of office sparkling on his chest. He was talking to the supermarket manager and a few other men in suits. Nigel and Barry were standing at the supermarket doors, staring menacingly at the crowd. Tom Henderson was bouncing up and down on the balls of his feet. He didn't seem to know how to stand still.

The supermarket manager led the provost up to the microphone, which had been set up in the middle of the red carpet.

'This is an exciting day for Rothiemuir,' boomed the provost. 'A major new shopping facility has come to our town with all the advantages of . . .'

But at that moment, the microphone stopped working. The provost didn't seem to notice. He went on talking, his mouth opening and shutting, but nobody could hear a word he was saying. Finn saw Nigel and Barry glance at each other, then look round uncertainly.

Jas grabbed Finn's arm and started jumping up and down, waving her arms to catch Kyla and Amir's attention. They saw her and hurried over. Amir looked triumphant. Kyla looked worried.

'Amir found the plug for the microphone,' said Kyla. 'He pulled it out. He'll get into awful trouble if anyone saw him.'

Amir smirked, pleased with himself.

'There's an extension cable. It was easy. It'll hold them up for a bit, anyway. What about Tom Henderson, Finn? Did you speak to him? What did he say?'

Finn simply shook his head. He couldn't bear to explain it all again.

The microphone spluttered back into life.

Amir looked disappointed.

'I thought it would take them ages to find the socket.' He shrugged. 'I tried, anyway.'

Finn wasn't listening. His eyes were fixed on a brilliant mass of yellow balloons, each one stamped with the name of the supermarket in bright scarlet letters. They were held in nets behind a chain-link fence with a gate in the middle of it.

'One minute to go!' shouted the supermarket manager. 'And then our legendary guest, the one and only Tom Henderson, is going to release the balloons and open the supermarket. The countdown has begun! Do it with me, everyone! Sixty! Fifty-nine! Fifty-eight!'

The crowd enthusiastically joined in.

'Fifty-seven! Fifty-six!'

Finn, watching in agony, became aware that Dougie, who had escaped from Mrs Lamb and had wriggled his way to them through the crowd, was tugging at Jas's sleeve.

'Jas, I've done something awful,' he said. 'I don't know what to do. You've got to help me.'

'Forty-three! Forty-two!' roared the crowd.

'What?' said Jas. 'Not now, Dougie.'

'I didn't mean to do it, honestly,' said Dougie. 'It was just that I was over there, where the balloons are, and there's this gate in the fence. I sort of wondered if my padlock would fit over the catch thing, and I sort of slipped it on, and then it snapped shut all by itself, and just to check that it was still working I spun the numbers and now I can't get it off again. I changed the number you make to undo it yesterday, and now

I can't remember what it is.'

'Thirty! Twenty-nine! Twenty-eight!'

'You silly . . .' began Jas automatically, then she stopped and stared down at him. 'Dougie, are you telling me that you've padlocked the gate where the balloons are and there's no way you can open it?'

'Yes,' said Dougie unhappily. 'What am I going to do, Jas? I didn't mean . . .'

'Twenty! Nineteen! Eighteen!'

Finn's head had jerked up. He felt as if a light had gone on in his head.

'Dougie, you're a genius!' he crowed. With a rush of strength that surprised him, he picked Dougie up and swung him round. Over the younger boy's head, he could see the supermarket manager walking over to the balloon enclosure. Now he was staring, horrified, at the locked padlock.

'Ten! Nine! Eight!' yelled the crowd.

The provost was leading Tom Henderson along the red carpet to the enclosure, where the manager, red in the face, was struggling desperately with Dougie's padlock.

'Five! Four! Three! Two! One!'

The crowd fell silent, waiting for the wonderful

sight of five thousand golden balloons rising up and filling the sky.

Nothing happened. Finn felt Jas's hand gripping his arm. Charlie was kneading his other shoulder.

'Oh!' said Dougie. 'I've just remembered the number! It's four, three, two, one! I'd better go and tell them.'

Five pairs of arms shot out and grabbed him.

'You're not going anywhere,' said Finn gleefully. 'Don't you get it, Dougie? You've saved the day!'

Chapter Sixteen

It took a moment or two for the crowd to realize that something had gone wrong, then the expectant silence gave way to impatient mutterings.

'What are they playing at?' people all round the children were saying. 'Do they want us to hang around here all day?'

'Never mind the balloons!' someone shouted at last. 'Open the doors! We want to go shopping!'

The six children had quietly edged round the side of the crowd towards the balloon enclosure to see what was going on. Mr Price, the supermarket manager, was red in the face with fury. He was trying to wrench the padlock off with his bare hands. The provost's mouth was set in a stiff smile as he nodded reassuringly at the crowd, pretending that everything was going according to plan. Tom Henderson's driver, Sam, had slipped up to the footballer and was whispering in his ear. Then he spoke quietly to the provost.

'Good idea!' boomed the provost, forgetting that he was still holding the microphone. 'Let's forget the balloons and get on with opening the shop.'

He took Mr Price by the elbow and forcefully steered him away from the balloons towards the yellow ribbon that was strung across the supermarket's closed doors.

'And now,' he went on, in his loud official voice, 'our distinguished guest, Mr Tom Henderson, is going to make a speech.'

Tom Henderson's jaw dropped open.

'A speech?' he whispered to Sam. 'What speech? No one said anything about a speech!

Charlie dug Finn in the ribs.

'What's he saying?'

Finn shrugged.

'I don't know, but he looks dead scared.'

Charlie shook his head.

'Tom Henderson? Scared? Nah! He's not scared of anything!'

*

There was no way out for the champion footballer. The microphone was thrust into his hands. He cleared his throat, looked wildly round, then gave an awkward smile as a cheer rippled round the crowd.

'Hello, everyone,' he said in a squeaky voice. 'Thanks a lot for coming.' He stopped and swallowed. 'Looks like you've got a . . . a nice new supermarket here. Hope it sells footballs, eh?'

He turned to look at Mr Price, who gave a tiny shake of his head and stared at the ground.

'Um – anyone see *Match of the Day* last night?' he went on. 'Fantastic goal wasn't it, in the second half?'

His eyes swivelled round the crowd as he desperately thought of something else to say. They fell upon Finn, who had been waving his arms like a windmill, hoping to catch his attention and remind him about the dolphins.

'Oh yes, about the balloons,' Tom went on. 'Sorry you're disappointed, but it's probably good, in a way. Balloons are bad for dolphins. It's to do with jellyfish . . . What? What do you want?'

He had turned to talk to Sam, who was whispering frantically in his ear. The crowd were starting to mutter again, exchanging puzzled looks.

Tom lifted the microphone to his mouth again.

'Tell you what, everyone, there's a boy over there. He'll explain. Come here, you. Finn, isn't it?'

Finn was so shocked to hear his name that for a moment he couldn't move. Then Jas gave him a shove in the back, and Amir said, 'Go on, man. This is it.'

Finn walked in a daze to the red carpet, but as he went, something began to happen. His mind calmed and his racing heart settled. He felt a surge of confidence. It was as if he was back in the sea among the dolphins. He wasn't Finn, the awkward lonely boy. He was magical Finn, the sea boy, who had swum in the deep water and leaped with the dolphins.

He took the microphone from Tom and turned to face the crowd.

'Thank you, Mr Price, for not releasing the balloons,' he heard himself say. 'People don't know, but they're really bad for animals in the sea. Lots of creatures like dolphins and turtles and everything think balloons are jellyfish. Birds do, too. Ask Professor Jamieson. He knows. They eat the balloons, and loads of other bits of plastic, bags and stuff. Their insides get filled up with rubbish and they starve. And they get tangled in the strings too.'

He paused as a new idea struck him.

'Balloons are more fun indoors, anyway. Why don't you get the nets inside your supermarket, Mr Price, and let them go there? Everyone can play with them!'

Mr Price, who had already had a terrible morning, looked as if he had just received the killer blow, but there were cheers from the crowd.

'Well said! Great idea!' people were shouting. 'How old are you, Finn? Bet you turn out to be prime minister one day.'

Finn looked round the crowd in a daze. He couldn't take it in. They'd done it! The faces melted into a blur, and as they did, Finn felt the sea boy inside him shrink away and disappear. He was turning once again into the old Finn, awkward and shy, who had never so much as raised his voice in class. His face flooded pink with embarrassment. He fled from the red carpet back to his friends, who had moved away from the balloon enclosure and were standing at the back of the crowd.

'Quick!' he said to Dougie. 'No one's looking. Go back and get your padlock off before anyone sees.'

Dougie grinned and patted his pocket,

making something metal clink.

'Done it already. I was clever, wasn't I, Finn? It was me, wasn't it? You said I'd saved the day.'

'Course you did, Dougie.' Finn realized suddenly that the others were all staring at him. 'What's the matter with you lot?'

'You were . . . different,' said Amir.

'Awesome,' said Kyla.

'Incredible,' said Charlie.

'Like you were in the sea, when you were leaping with the dolphins,' said Jas.

'I'm glad you're in the Lighthouse Crew now, Finn,' said Kyla. 'Are you really going to be prime minister? You wouldn't like it. You'd have to live in London. The traffic's awful. It's really dangerous.'

The microphone crackled on again.

'This is the moment we've all been waiting for!' said the provost. 'Tom Henderson is going to cut the ribbon and open the doors!'

There was a fumbling noise as the microphone was handed over. Then Tom Henderson announced, 'I now declare this supermarket open!'

Charlie grabbed Amir's arm.

'Quick! He'll be going in a moment. Let's get over there and get his autograph!'

The crowd was rapidly piling through the open doors, leaving the car park empty.

'Watch out, Dougie,' murmured Jas. 'Here comes your mum.'

'Dougie!' Mrs Lamb's face was pink with annoyance. 'Where have you been? I've been looking for you everywhere! You mustn't slip off like that. I've told you again and again. You nagged me into bringing you, and I wish I'd never given in.'

'It's all right, Mrs Lamb,' said Jas. 'He was with us all the time.'

'Well, I hope you've kept him out of mischief,' she said, looking at her suspiciously.

Jas stared back at her innocently.

'He's been as good as gold, hasn't he, Kyla?'

'Good as gold,' repeated Kyla.

'We'd better go and find our dads, too,' said Jas to Finn, as Mrs Lamb dragged Kyla and Dougie away.

'No need to go far.' Finn nodded towards the provost, who was still standing on the red carpet. Professor Jamieson was engaging him in earnest conversation, while Mr McFee stood well back, as if he was uneasy being in such exalted company.

Finn and Jas hurried up to them.

'Ah,' said the professor, turning to Finn. 'Here's

the young man who made such a stirring speech! How old are you, Finn?'

Finn looked at the ground, embarrassed.

'Eleven.'

'Remarkable,' said the provost. He turned back to the professor. 'So it's your opinion, Professor, that the council should impose a blanket ban on mass balloon releases?'

'It is, yes.' Professor Jamieson put his hands in his pockets and began to jingle his change, a sure sign that he was about to launch into a speech. 'The scientific evidence, collected from a significant number of sources, shows that—'

'Dad,' said Jas.

'What?' Professor Jamieson turned. 'Yes, quite right, my dear. I mustn't go on, but the provost and I were just—'

'I'll certainly bring the matter up at the next council meeting for discussion. Perhaps you would like to come and present evidence, Professor? *Brief* evidence? I really had no idea, you know, that balloons were . . . Of course, we're all aware now that plastic pollution's a problem in the sea. I'm glad to say that there'll be no free plastic bags at this supermarket, anyway! Well . . .'

Finn had stopped listening and gone over to his father.

'Why are you looking at me like that, Dad?' he said.

Mr McFee was rubbing his eyes. Tears glistened on his cheeks.

'It's you, son. When you were up there, standing so tall, saying all that, I was so proud of you. I didn't know what to do with myself. And you looked like her. Just like her. The light in your eyes . . .'

'Let's get out of here,' said Finn, who was suddenly desperate to get away. 'Let's go home to Stromhead.'

'Will you take me too, Mr McFee?' asked Jas, who had given up trying to get her father away from the provost. 'I can tell that Dad's going to be ages.'

No one said much on the drive back to Stromhead. Mr McFee dropped Jas and Finn at the top of the beach and went off to fill the van with petrol.

Finn stood looking out to sea, breathing in the rich salt smell. The sun shimmered on the rippling surface of the water. Its reflection made a golden path, which seemed to invite him in. Was that the flick of a tail he could see, moving far out from the shore? Was that the shadow of a creature swimming below the surface? He felt the call of his other friends – his dolphin friends – and he needed to answer it.

'Will you come to the lantern room tomorrow, Finn?' asked Jas. 'We can't stop our campaign yet! I was talking to Dad last night. There's loads more things we can do. That we've *got* to do!'

Finn grinned at her.

'I know. I was thinking about that. We need a planning meeting. The Lighthouse Crew cleaning up the sea, eh, Jas?'

She smiled back at him, but before she could say anything more, he turned to look longingly out to sea and said, 'I've got to go now. Tell my dad I'll find my own way home.'

She didn't need to ask where he was going.

'I wish I could come with you,' was all she said.

He nodded.

'I wish you could, too.'

'Be careful out there, Finn.'

He flashed her a smile.

'No need to worry. The sea's my friend. I'm quite safe in her. I feel as if I'm going home.'

And before she could say another word, he sprinted down to the water's edge.

Author's Note

Song of the Dolphin Boy began its life in France, when I was staying with some old friends. Thank you, Robin and Merril! Robin's nephew, Simon Christopher, was staying too. He makes underwater films of marine wildlife in Borneo, and he told me how worried he was about the state of the oceans. Thank you, Simon, for inspiring me.

We humans have used the seas as dumping grounds for all our waste for thousands of years. In the old days much of our rubbish just rotted or eroded harmlessly away, but then plastic was invented.

We all love plastic! We wrap our food in it, we use it to make our bright, colourful toys, our computers and phones, and almost anything else you can imagine. When we're tired of all our stuff, we just throw it away. You'd be amazed how much plastic rubbish ends up in the sea — around eight million tons a year — and there it stays. Vast islands of plastic that will last for thousands of years float about in the once-clean water. Whales, dolphins, seals and birds get tangled up in them. They think that plastic is food, and when they eat it their stomachs fill up, and they can starve.

I wanted to do something about this. I went to see Professor Paul Thompson, who runs the brilliant Aberdeen University Lighthouse Field Station in Cromarty. He told me about the problems caused by balloons when they're released into the air. They nearly always end up in the sea and can seriously harm dolphins and other wildlife. So thank you, Professor Thompson, for giving me the idea behind *Song of the Dolphin Boy*. And thank you too to Barbara Cheney, who shared her great knowledge of dolphins with me.

I hope you've enjoyed reading *Song of the Dolphin Boy*. You might feel inspired to look online to find out more about ocean conservation and the CleanSeas campaign. We humans need to care for our great, blue, beautiful oceans and all the wonderful animals and fish who live in them. We need to get the great clean-up started!

About the Author

Elizabeth Laird is the multi-award-winning author of several much-loved children's books. She has been shortlisted for the prestigious CILIP Carnegie Medal six times. She lives in Britain now, but still likes to travel as much as she can.